WHO ONLY LOOKS AT THE SEA

WHO ONLY LOOKS AT THE SEA

BY TIMOTHY HOFFELDER

WINDY CITY PUBLISHERS

WHO ONLY LOOKS AT THE SEA
© 2018 by Timothy Hoffelder

This book is a work of fiction. Names and characters are either products of the author's imagination or used fictitiously. Any resemblance to actual persons is coincidental. Additionally, most place names are real, but a few have been changed to protect the privacy of certain communities.

All rights reserved. No part of this publication may be reproduced or transmitted in any form or by any means, electronic or mechanical, including photocopy, recording, or any information storage and retrieval system, without permission in writing from the publisher.

Please contact publisher for permission to make copies of any part of this work.

Windy City Publishers
2118 Plum Grove Road, #349
Rolling Meadows, IL 60008
www.windycitypublishers.com

Published in the United States of America

ISBN#:
978-1-941478-58-5

Library of Congress Control Number:
2017962732

WINDY CITY PUBLISHERS
CHICAGO

This novel is dedicated to women and girls
who have much to teach the world
through their lived truth.

Likewise, it is dedicated to sharing
the healing and empowering potential of stories.

ACKNOWLEDGMENTS

With deepest gratitude to Philbert "Bart Michoro" Banzie
who provided the original cover art.

Additional thanks to Michael D. Acid,
Andre Vidal, Motolani Akinola, Kelsey Gordon,
and all those who supported the process of this story
finding its way into print.

TUESDAY EVENING

ON THE ISLAND OF UNGUJA in the Indian Ocean, there is a beach named Kiwimbi. All of the locals know the beach by this name, but I suppose the visitors and tourists do not. This is why I tell you its name now in case this is your first visit. Visitors might know it by another name. They may not care to ask for its name at all. I am unsure because I have never asked them, and they have never asked me.

Each morning before sunrise, local people exercise on Kiwimbi. Before these morning exercises take place, there are occasional Hindu cremations and there are daily returns of fishing boats. After the ashes have departed into the same wind which brings the tired fisherman ashore the exercises begin.

On Kiwimbi, there are jogging teams and capoeira teams. There are also individuals who do not belong to any team. These solitary swimmers and jumpers defy custom, but surely they rejoin the fold upon completion of their routine.

At Kiwimbi beach, there is also a track for running, a court for netball, a court for basketball, and a field for football. You may know this final sport as soccer, or you may know it as football. Perhaps even better, you know it as *mpira*. Perhaps this is not truly better, just different. Anyway, every evening before it is time for dinner these fields fill again with people. These evening exercises comprise running and jumping, and playing those sports with teams. Again, some people do not belong to any team. I do not know what those people want.

This evening, the sun is particularly early to sleep. On Unguja, we are close to the equator. Our daily supply of sunlight is nearly equal all year long. But, our island lies just south of the equator and this means that July is a little darker and very much cooler than other months. This evening, the sun is low on the water. It is as low as it may go without being fully swallowed by the waves. A blue like peacock feathers spreads across the sky, and the pink of bougainvillea flowers accompanies it. The sun itself is red like a dying ember.

On Unguja, we call this dark but colorful time *magharibi*. Travelers love this time, and they swarm Africa House to drink alcohol and take photos of the vision. Sometimes, these travelers venture out onto the beach, loosely wrapped in lacy scarves.

When they do, I ask them why they are so compelled to photograph the sunset on Unguja, and they always respond in the same way. They look at me with wonder and it is clear that my question is foolish to them. I know this because amusement is visible in their blue eyes like the kind reserved for clever children who ask surprising questions.

After they look at me for a moment, they explain how very beautiful this sunset is. They tell me that it is unlike anything else in the world. This is a funny thing to say, but I take them by their word. Yes, they must know the world better than me. After all, by their being here, they have at least seen their homes and Unguja and maybe more. Based on what they say, perhaps Unguja is unusual. Perhaps this makes me unusual, too! Me, I would not mind that.

I would not mind if the travelers think that I am an unusual girl. Unusual people are always the most interesting, and unusual things tend to be the most exciting. For example, I have lost count of how many times I have eaten maize porridge in my life. Thus, maize porridge is not unusual and I can confidently tell you that it is not exciting. I am not sure it has ever been exciting for me, to be honest, even the first time. Anyway, since I eat it so often it is not unusual and there is no excitement when it presents itself at lunchtime.

Now, when *biriyani* appears that is unusual indeed. *Biriyani* is a treat. Its saffron colors the rice so nicely. Its tamarind sauce makes for especially tasty fingerfuls of meat. Since *biriyani* arrives so rarely, my sisters and I love it even more. You see, because it is unusual, it brings a special joy. Like this, I would not mind being the unusual person. Unusual people can bring excitement or joy. That is a good thing, I think.

Do not misunderstand me, usual things are important in their own way. Maize porridge is less expensive than *biriyani*, and it is very filling. When I eat it, I become satisfied quite quickly. What it lacks in joy, it provides in energy. Likewise, usual people can be good, too. In fact, the ordinary people who grace my life every day after day are part of the reason that unusual people are so interesting. How do I know what is special and interesting if I do not have the ordinary to compare it with? It is not possible. In fact, just now I spend my time with some usual people.

At present, I sit with two friends a distance south of where the travelers drink alcohol and photograph the sun. My friends and I, we are sitting at Kiwimbi on the beach side of the airport road. Today, we have finished our last exams. Well, Asha and I have—one more remains for Khadija. I think that this is the reason for her sour mood now. It is not unusual, though, for her mood to turn sour without obvious reason. I do not expect you to think of Khadija as a friend, but I have known her for a very long time. To neglect her would be to deny too much. Thus, even through her sourest moments I sit with her like this. She is my sister.

Beneath our feet here, the sand is cool and dense. I know this because I am barefoot after having placed my sandals cleverly under my bottom for sitting. Khadija has done the same. Asha is especially clever and keeps her shoes while sitting instead on today's copy of *Nipashe*. The newspaper is a reliably good option for sitting on the sand, apart from the grease stains I observe on Asha's paper. I think she has repurposed a paper which has already been repurposed once for carrying lunch. But anyway, the coolness of the sand is also not unusual. This is the way sand becomes on July evenings.

On these evenings, breezes arrive and blow cool air from the South. The tall, tall palms and the short, fat baobabs wiggle in the air. This cool air confuses the ocean which trembles and stirs. Sometimes, the ocean waves grow large and unpredictable. Our aunties warn that June-July is an especially bad time to travel by ferry.

If you must go to Dar es Salaam, they say, wait until September. If you must go now and right now, they say, find money for a plane ticket—or at least, find money for a good ferry—perhaps Azam. Oh, but sit outside on the deck. Fresh air helps to settle somersaulting tummies. And, God forbid you must go to Pemba. That can surely wait.

Asha, Khadija, and me, we like to sit here next to the airport road on days like this. December or February days are too, too hot. Those days, we stay indoors or under the shade of trees, but a July evening is an especially good time to sit quietly together until darkness falls and it is time to go home or risk a shouting from Auntie. We like sitting here because it helps get a fresh mind after long days.

Also, it is quite liberating to sit idly in pleasant air surrounded by activity. Football players race across the field, kicking up dust. A small child is collecting discarded bottles to clean and fill with juice. Later, he probably helps his mother to sell it. Elder men are drinking coffee next to a phone credit man. Here, there are no stray cats like in Stonetown. This is a good thing, because those cats, I tell you, they have mites and bad parasite worms. Still, they demand attention and come too close. The bravest ones even touch their faces to our ankles. But, at Kiwimbi there are no cats. Behind us, drivers are returning home at uncomfortable speeds. We are safe here away from the road, but each time that they roar past they challenge our safety and the little hairs on our arms tingle with alarm. It feels exciting in a naughty way.

More than the lack of cats or the exciting, tingling feeling, I simply like Kiwimbi's activity because it is easy to watch. I have learned after years of life that I have a talent for watching. This is a talent a person can have, I assure you.

Whereas Asha and Khadija sit surrounded by meaningless activity, I am sitting surrounded by observable fascinations. I read them like a book. For example, Asha probably does not realize that the small child collects plastic bottles so that he can sell juice in them later. Khadija surely does not know that the drivers travel at tremendous speeds because they are late for dinner once again and their first wives will insist with barbed words that perhaps they eat at their second wives' homes and be done with the matter.

But me, I know these things because I have a talent for watching. A person can know a lot about someone else just by looking at them with great focus. Asha and Khadija do not care to do this because they find it boring. Me, I think they are boring. What is not boring, however, is the moments when people are unusual. These people are the most interesting of all, since they challenge me to think with lots of focus in order to understand them.

At this moment, for example, I am watching one of those boys who does not belong to any team. As I have explained already, this is ordinary. There are always a few people who exercise alone, away from the teams of joggers or swimmers. Thus, what the boy is doing here is not so unusual, but who the boy is being here is quite unusual.

You see, this boy is a white boy. I know this because I can see it. His skin, his hair, and even the way he picks up his feet and puts them back down are what I can see and I have determined all of them to be white. Here, we call boys like him an *mzungu*. This is just what they are called.

The first time I saw an *mzungu*, I was a very little girl. I do not remember this moment, but I can also never forget it. I cannot forget it because my mother will not let me. She will tell the story whenever and wherever the story may fit. If there were a few minutes before bedtime, she may tell the story. If there were many minutes before the bus came, she may tell the story then, too.

The first time I saw an *mzungu*, my cheeks were very round—like a monkey! We have monkeys on Unguja, you know. We call them *punju*, or Red Colobus. They eat all day and they fart all night, and the *wazungu* love them very much. And, the monkeys do not mind the *wazungu*. However, despite my looking like a monkey I am told that I did mind very much the *mzungu* when I met him for that first time. The white man in question was from England, and he was an English language teacher. The British government decided that he was fit to give advice to the Revolutionary Government of Zanzibar's Ministry of Education. This is what brought him to Unguja. What brought him to my home was an invitation from my auntie. I suppose she was being polite, and he was, too, and suddenly they were eating a meal together because it was the polite thing to do.

The first time I saw an *mzungu*, the face I made was not the polite thing to do, no. When the English teacher held that little, monkey-cheeked me carefully in his lap, wrapped in a blue and yellow *kanga*—as my mother may tell you—my round eyes looked at his different face and my little ears heard his different voice. I tell you—as my mother may tell you—I screamed, and cried, and frightened that white man so. In his heart, he knew that I cried in fear because I knew him to be different. And, this is not a pleasant feeling: to be so different that you cause crying. Oh, he was sorry to hold that little baby girl who was me.

Now, this time when I see an *mzungu* at Kiwimbi I am not startled. At least, I am not startled in the same way a baby girl is startled. I do not scream or cry, *namshukuru Mungu*. Baby girls with round, monkey cheeks make for funny stories which aunties and mothers can tell. But, young ladies who shout and cry out because of different faces are not so funny. This is what I tell my friend when she also sees the white boy exercising alone.

"*Huyo*! Have you seen him, hee!" Khadija pulls her scarf over her chin, making her mouth quite small, and she laughs with her wide eyes. If you have not seen a Swahili girl laugh with her eyes, then you must see it to understand this thing which she does now.

"Look at him," she points with her lips, so that our friend Asha and I may see. If you have not seen a Swahili girl point with her lips, then you may not understand this thing either. It is more subtle than the kizungu way of pointing with long fingers, but it is pointing, nonetheless.

Asha looks, too. She curiously watches the *mzungu* man run on the sand track with his nice shoes. She says something about those nice shoes.

"Oh stop it, you," I say. I wave my hand like a broom, sweeping away their dusty issues.

They look at me, surprised. Eyebrows rise.

"Hee, *weye*! Nothing new to you, is it?"

"No, maybe she must see white gentlemen every week at Bwawani Club. This is not new for her!"

My friends cackle. No one cares to cover themselves shyly this time. Instead, the laugh quickly swells to uncontainable joy, together they delightfully squeal ah!-haaaah, and they slap hands victoriously.

This is another way Swahili girls laugh sometimes. If you have not seen it, then you are lucky. If you have, it means that you are either very funny like a comedian or very funny like an ugly fish. People do not usually want to be the second kind of funny.

I cannot find words to respond to their evil joke, so I simply give them silence. My knees straighten, legs stand, and my proud feet carry me in the direction of the track. I hear an astonished 'hebu!' from behind me. They are expecting me to sit and endure their friendly torture. They have not expected me to rise up courageously and abandon them.

To be truthful with you, I have not expected this, either. Me, I am not really a courageous girl. I do not even normally talk to strangers, and particularly not foreign ones. I enjoy very much watching strangers since they are unusual and interesting—just not talking with them.

I suppose my feet are more courageous than my head, because my ears feel hot with anger at Khadija and my brow sweats with fear at how close I come to the track, but my feet continue. That is it. They have taken command now, these feet of mine. My eyes and my hands are not to be heard while my feet lead us all into imminent, shameful doom.

Finally, the rest of my body steals the blood back away from my cavalier legs and we all collapse onto a small bench at the edge of the sandy track. From the safety of this slab of driftwood my head turns to peak at the girls behind me, and they are both smiling in the first way I have told you that Swahili girls sometimes smile. That is, their mouths are very small and their eyes are very big. I understand them to be restraining laughter at me. So, I turn back away from them and I look at the sea.

The *mzungu* man passes my line of vision. He is still running, and I see now that his shoes are very nice—it is true. I note to myself that I am not going to tell Asha how nice his shoes are. She is silly, and I cannot concede to her. I do not think I can lie, but I can change the topic if she mentions it.

Maybe you have seen running shoes like this white man's shoes, but I cannot say that I have before now. They are white, the color of silver, and the color of sapphires. The white color is so bright and the other colors shine in such a way that I know something else about this man. Yes, either he must polish his shoes very nicely or he has not been in Africa for very long. Oh, but maybe he has a mother or an auntie who polishes his shoes. And, maybe he lives in a gated home like those ones in Chukwani with their marble floors and crystal lamps. Those ones always seem to be dust-free, somehow. Hm, I suppose I do not know as much as I have thought about this *mzungu*.

Anyway, it is true that his shoes are very nice. His hair is also nice, I think. While it is dark like an Indian man's hair, it is more silky—like a woman's! This thought causes me to cover my mouth and widen my eyes in the way Swahili girls laugh sometimes.

As my eyes are laughing, the *mzungu* is suddenly in front of me. He has stopped running, and he is standing in front of me, oh, no.

"Sorry," he says.

But, he says it in Swahili: *samahani*.

My wide eyes grow wider. He sees this and laughs politely. Then, he greets me, saying '*hujambo dada*.' I feel my lips replying '*sijambo*' behind my closed fingers. The '*-ja-*' syllable seems to have landed higher than it is accustomed to doing, crashing back down to a very quiet '*-mbo*' afterward. Oh, I am nervous. Why is he talking to me?

"I am exercising here, but I do not have my phone and so I do not know the time. My sister, do you know the time?"

The words leave his pale, pink lips and arrive at my green scarf where they find my covered, brown ears. When they leave the foreign lips, they must have danced a strange dance in the island air because after their trip through the air, you see, they arrive to my ears as words which do not sound foreign at all. No, this *mzungu* sounds like my neighbors. He has no *kizungu* accent. I look at him more fully.

On his face, there are a few marks like pimples or little spots. His nose is big, which is not so different here. But, his skin is light-light light almost like he is mixed blood—but a mixture into which its Maker has spilled some lightening cream. This lightness is why I determine him to be *mzungu*, but now that he is standing so close to my eyes, I am unsure. His hair is an Indian lady's, his nose is a Saudi man's, his pimples are an *mzungu's*, and his words are Swahili. What an unusual human he is, here at Kiwimbi.

I resolve to take notes about this man and his unusual mixture later.

"Do you know the time?"

Owh! I pull my *tochi* phone from my pocket. It is 12 hours and 20 minutes, and I tell him so. I see in his eyes that he is thinking about this, and then he nods his head.

"*Nakushukuru,*" he thanks me.

In school, I have learned that most *wazungu* do not learn the proper way to tell time in school—not even at home! You see, they wake up and the day has already begun without them. In fact, it begins in the middle of the night right around six-hours nighttime. My mother would tell you that this is why they are so punctual. She will say that *if you woke each day to find that six or even seven hours have gone by without you, then you would care very much about not being late, too*! My mother can be a funny lady, yes.

While I am thinking about my mother, the *mzungu* boy, he crosses the airport road into Kikwajuni. I watch him do this, and I see Khadija and Asha watching, too. Then, they look at me with big eyes. They are surprised, and I am, too. But, I do not let them see my surprise because they are sillier than me.

"Where is that one going?"

"He is already lost!"

I suggest that, "Maybe he lives here, in Kikwajuni."

Khadija snorts and Asha giggles.

"Maybe! But why don't you go and ask him!"

My face becomes warm and I scowl at them. They like to tease me because they know me. This is what friends do, isn't it? Friends, they know you best and so they know the best ways to make you itch.

"The sun has set," I observe aloud, and begin my journey home.

Asha and Khadija, they join me, but I think they know that like the sunlight, my patience for their teasing has reached its limit for the day.

Patience—even with friends—is a funny thing. Just like the daylight, it seems to be everlasting and obvious, until suddenly it does not exist at all. Of course, it does always return after some darkness.

Here on Unguja, in case you do not know, daylight is much like patience in this way. We have it in abundance—sometimes overabundance. The sun can be very mean here, I tell you!

Then, at just about 12 hours daytime, we have none at all. Particularly now as Ramadhan approaches and the moon is absent, it is even darker. The sun sets, the stars alight, and it is very dark indeed. I know this because I have visited Dar es Salaam before.

There in the big city, when the electricity is working, you cannot see stars like here on the islands. There in the city, lights and patience are not so much the same. Rather, I think they have much more light, but much less patience.

I wonder if the *mzungu* who runs has more light or more patience in the place where he comes from. Perhaps he has less of both. I think this is probably the case, because many *wazungu* who come to Unguja are demanding, impatient people, but their skin is so light that it burns and crackles in the island sun. Such skin cannot be accustomed to abundant light, or else it would not burn so readily each time in this way. This *mzungu* who runs does not have burnt, crackling skin. Maybe he stays indoors reading, or perhaps he covers himself when he is not exercising at Kiwimbi.

These many thoughts distract my mind while my feet carry on dutifully toward Auntie's house. When I arrive, I wish Asha and Khadija a good evening. It is time for me to be at my home and for them to be at theirs, and I know that this is understood. They walk on, toward the blockish tower flats of Michenzani. That is where they live.

Me, I slip in through the courtyard door. I do not even announce my presence because I know that no one is home for the moment. I have not shared this knowledge with Asha and Khadija because they would have offered to stay with me until family arrived. It is not proper for one to sit all alone, especially in the evening. Not even sick people spend their time alone. It is unusual behavior— of criminals and depressed people.

For now, it is just me while the others are visiting our cousin in Jang'ombe. Auntie likes to cook for cousins when they are not feeling well. She knows a recipe with beans and corn in whose healing powers she places full confidence. This recipe comes from Iringa on the mainland. That is where Auntie's mother comes from, too.

Oh! My feet sidestep a scraggly kitten who suddenly appears from behind a wash basin. This one is here, no doubt, because my younger brother has scooped it up from some place and brought it home. It does not matter. He is careless, my brother.

Inside, nobody is home, as expected. It is only me and scraggly kitten, I see. As long as that one does not cry or make noises like sad kittens do, then I do not mind. I kick off my sandals, and my tired feet find their way to my sister's dresser. In the bottom drawer, under aging socks, inside a particularly old sock that no one would purposefully select, is where I keep my notepad. Most days, I keep it with me. All other times, it hides here in this oldest sock.

My notepad itself, it is a blue color—the color of deep, deep waters. I refer to the places in the sea where your feet are not even visible below you and you must know how to swim. Those places terrify me. Nobody chooses to be in a place like that. No, that color is learned by accident; if one has fallen from a boat, or found herself too far out when the tide is high. That is the color of my notepad. On a notepad, it is much less intimidating. I like that I can hold it in my hand. In my hand, it is not terrifying. In fact, it is just paper.

I open the deep, dark waters-colored paper cover and fold it back. I have had other notepads like this one in other colors and sizes. Those ones that are full, they are not as important as this one. That is because the older notepads are full of things I have written as a young, young girl. Now, I am older, and the things I write are more interesting.

Mostly, I write the stories of the ones I see. For example, the *mzungu* who runs at Kiwimbi, he has an unusual story, and so he is fitting to write about in my notepad. Accordingly, my fingers flick through a few pages until they find where I have finished my last. Page 20, this is the next blank space. My pen entitles it Page 20—*the* mzungu *who runs*.

Normally, I take notes about the ones I see. I mean to say, I write their stories while I watch them. This time, my notepad has been here away from me, so I forgive myself for taking some notes in—what is that one Asha sometimes says to sound clever? It is *after-the-fact*! Yes.

After-the-fact, my pen scratches at the cream-colored paper. It begins to describe the *mzungu* who runs: *tall, but not very, very tall, a full head higher than me, but still smaller in stature than our cousins from Pemba…dark hair which looks soft and wavy like an Indian lady…light-light skin, but not that kind which reddens and suffers in the light…a nose which commands attention—a regal nose—I have not seen the Sultan of Oman, but I do think he has a nose like this one…but, I know that he is not fully Arab in his blood…*

It is too unusual for Arab men to have little marks all over their nose and cheeks like this *mzungu* who runs. The ones from Europe, they have those little brown spots like dear siblings in permanent accompaniment. We Africans keep many children in our families, but very few spots; while the Europeans, they keep few children but many little spots. Humans are balanced in this way, you see. One who has little of one thing has much of another. *Aso hilo ana lile*: she without this has that.

My pen waits for a moment while my thoughts finish. It begins again.

The mzungu *who runs is of mixed blood. He has a Spanish mother and an Arab father…Ah, but…his father's father is Indian. And, his mother's father is English. This is what makes him look the way he looks…As for what makes him sound the way he sounds…He has learned Swahili—the Swahili of Unguja, of Kikwajuni and Kiwimbi…He has learned it because his government has paid him to do this.*

Governments, they do that. I know because we have learned it in our civics class. First, they collect money from all of their citizens. Then, they count the money. Based on the total, they make grand plans for this and for that. They give five percent to schools and nine percent to pensions. They often give a very large percent to policemen and military, and they give a similarly large percent to themselves.

Anyway, these grand plans which they call budgets typically give some amount to citizens who want to do clever things in the world. I have told you about the *mzungu* English teacher from my childhood. He belongs in this category. His government gave him money to go far away, give advice to us local people and learn about culture and ways. Then, he can go back and share what he has learned. The government can have a better idea of other places and peoples. It can make decisions based on this. It is like an investment, you see, and this is why it gets to be in a budget next to pensions and policemen.

Similarly, *the* mzungu *who runs has been given budgeted money. His government has sent him to Zanzibar to learn Swahili. But, of course, they have sent him to learn about Zanzibari culture and ways. Then, he can return to his government and tell them what he has learned. They will be happy because they have invested in him wisely.*

But, his country and his government—which one does he come from exactly?

After all, I do not think it matters. Most *wazungu* are the same, even if they first seem to be unusual like this one.

I close my notepad and replace it there, wrapped inside the oldest sock.

WEDNESDAY MORNING

IN THE HEART OF STONETOWN, Mji Mkongwe, there is a place we call Jaws Corner. In this clearing of our stone jungle, men gather to play checkers and listen to political news. The news plays on televisions attached to awnings and tall poles. It plays on radios, too. Elders drink coffee and young men cut hair. Sometimes, wazungu ladies drink coffee, too. These are brave, enigmatic ladies. Girls like me, we do not drink coffee with the men of Jaws Corner. We drink chai, and we drink it at home. Sometimes when we are fortunate we drink it at our friends' homes, and when we are very fortunate we drink it at Forodhani after sunset while the waves play noisily on the old wall.

However, at Jaws Corner, no, I do not drink coffee here. Instead, I sit on a stoop just outside the main clearing. I suppose you may call it Jaws Corner's Corner—my corner. In my corner, I sit stooped on a *baraza*. I share it with courageous cats who beg for scraps and all the small children who pass by and sit for a while. A tailor works inside, just beyond the threshold of this stoop. He deftly shears *kanga* and *kitenge* into long shapes. These shapes, he places them strategically and seams them together with his machine, *shu-shu-shu*. Like magic, they transform into dresses, jackets, trousers. As his heavy scissors do their work, little pieces of fabric fall away floorward, like crumbs from an impossibly colorful meal. The courageous cats sometimes inspect these crumbs, but learning that they are indeed inedible, they return to the stoop by my side.

From my corner, I can watch the elders drink coffee from little, porcelain cups for 100 shillings. They play *bao*, dominoes, and checkers. Pieces dance with fingers on wooden boards, *pa-pa-pap*. Though I cannot see the TV screens, I also hear their boisterous dramas. At home, my mother's TV may feature

Indian or Venezuelan families. These families like to betray each other and quarrel. At Jaws Corner, the TV sets exclusively feature two dramas but neither includes quarrelsome families, just quarrelsome men: impassioned speeches by the Civic United Front—CUF for short—or the English Premier League.

CUF and the Premier League, they are not so different. One comprises men who battle with words, and the other with feet. Both wear uniforms. Both seek to represent their country. From my corner, I do not mind that I cannot view the TV screens or the dramatic men they feature. This is because I watch the ones who watch the screens.

From my corner, I do my favorite thing. This thing is taking notes. I have already told you about my notepad and its profoundly blue cover. Now, let me tell you about its contents. It is not the same notetaking which students do during a lecture. That type of notetaking requires no thinking. It is simple conversion of text to voice to pen and to text again: a funny thing, that. Sometimes, the teacher even reads aloud straight from her reference text. Why we cannot read for ourselves and copy what we see, I do not know. But, teachers are not ones to be questioned. Many times, I suppose there are not enough reference texts whereby each learner may privately read her own, anyway.

To be truthful with you, my notetaking is more like the notetaking policemen do when they investigate a crime scene. I know this because I have seen officers doing such things in Darajani market and on the Indian dramas. Like me, they have small notepads for writing. Like me, they look carefully at all the people and the things around them. But unlike me, they ask people questions.

I must tell you that I do not talk to the ones about whom I take notes. The *mzungu* who runs is a special case, but even then I am not the one who begins the talking. Indeed, talking is not productive whatsoever for this task. I have tried to watch interesting people while sitting with Khadija before. It is not possible. Khadija likes to talk. She asks me about what it is that I write. This is a distraction. When I have occasionally shared with her she has even dared to disagree with my notes, oh! Then, as she knows who it is that I watch she begins to watch those people, too. She continues to voice her opinions, which I tell you are not helpful. For this reason, I prefer to sit alone when I am watching and taking notes.

Now, the small children do not cause a problem. They, the cats, and the tailor do not distract me. They are okay. With their quiet chatter vaguely on my ears, and the tailor's humming machine *shu-shu-shu*, I am still able to look at all the people and the things like a good policeman detective and I make notes.

For example, now I watch one certain elder who sits alone. Though he is next to the coffee vendors, he does not speak with them. In fact, he does not drink coffee at all. He does not engage in games of *bao* or checkers, either. This is unusual for elderly men in Jaws Corner. Unusual things are premium notes, you see, so I take aim at this *mzee* who does not drink coffee or play games, and I look at him carefully.

Mzee Hanywi Kahawa, as I have named him in my notes, Page 21, wears the same colors every day. I have noticed this. He dresses in traditional Muslim style, with floor-length *kanzu*, brown sandals, and a *kofia* on his head. Mzee Kahawa wears his *kofia* unfolded so that it stands at its full height like—hmm—like a funny cloth flower pot on his head, ha ha! His grey hairs, of which I note there are many for such a very old man—another unusual thing!—are wispy vines, spilling out from the overturned vessel. Even this style of hat is unusual for elders.

Many times when the young boys wear their *kofia* like this, their uncles scold them, snatching the hat and folding it down proper. But, I note by his appearance that Mzee Kahawa likely does not have uncles to scold him these days. This *mzee* barely even has teeth these days. I note that only one large bottom tooth is visible. Though he does not drink coffee, I surmise that Mzee Kahawa has liked sweets very much in his lifetime. This explains the missing teeth.

Mzee Hanywi has worn the same outfit every day since the passing of his third wife: kanzu *the color of cream, brown sandals, and brown* kofia *atop his head…Mzee Hanywi does not drink coffee, and he does not play games…he does like sweets. He likes them very much. His favorites are the lemon-flavored ones… this love of sweets has rotted away all his teeth but one: a lone tooth on the bottom row…well, it cannot truly be a row without more than one, hm…Mzee Hanywi*

Kahawa has an age of 95 years. He is nearly as old as the famous Bi. Kidude, but not quite...In fact, his sister and Bi. Kidude are dear friends. When the singer travels to Dar, Mzee Kahawa's sister accompanies her. She does not go with her on tours to Europe, though. Their friendship does not extend quite that far.

Mzee Kahawa is a special type of old. As recorded in my notepad, Page 22, he is very thin. His skin is African brown, but like milky *chai*. A person can see that he comes from a different time. He and his milky *chai* skin do not come from a time of revolutionary government, but before then of just revolutionary whispers. My mother would tell you that elders like Mzee Kahawa are to be especially respected—for many reasons, of course—but also because they have seen much more than we can imagine.

My mother would tell you that he has seen many different Zanzibars and many different worlds, but through all these changes, Mzee Kahawa has stayed right here; sitting at Jaws Corner—his corner. Despite his small frame, he is as ancient and knowing as a great, big baobab 100 times his size. Behind round spectacles, his drooping eyes have seen all the changes. With his floppy, elephant ears he has heard all the dramas, political as well as athletic. I wonder if anything is new to him these days. Perhaps he knows everything there is to know in this life. Yes, I think he does.

At 95 years of age, Mzee Kahawa moves slowly. Sudden movements do not suit his frail body...His body is very thin. Granted, it has never been plump, but now it is especially thin in his old age. He uses a sturdy, wooden cane to prop himself up, even while sitting...skin is African brown...like milky chai. *Evidently, he is of mixed Arab and Bantu blood, but this is not unusual.*

In fact, nothing about Mzee Hanywi Kahawa's physical appearance is unusual or noteworthy. Rather, as I have mentioned to you, it is his choice of interaction—or non-interaction, owh, is there a word for that?—which makes him stand out to me. This, and perhaps the funny way he wears his hat, are what demonstrate him to be unusual.

Mzee Kahawa leans sleepily into his cane now. His gaze stays fixed on a particular spot just in front of him, in the middle of Jaws Corner. No one sits in this spot. There is no television or radio there. What are you looking at, *mzee*?

Suddenly, I observe that Mzee Kahawa is no longer looking at his preferred looking spot in the middle of the square. Perhaps he looks at children sitting beside me on the stoop. Perhaps the tailor has come out to stand in the doorway, and he has drawn attention to himself? No, he looks at me! I drop my pen in my notepad and close it shut. His gaze holds, and I tell you, Mzee Kahawa extends his right hand and beckons me.

If you have not seen the way a Swahili person beckons another, then I will tell you how we do it. Like Mzee Kahawa does now, we reach our hand forward with palm facing outward, and we bend all the fingers down to the palm.

It is funny, sometimes *wazungu* ladies do this when they mean to greet little children from far away, but of course seeing this gesture the children run forward and confusion ensues when the children are no longer far away but very, very close. The ladies become flustered. *Wazungu* ladies are strange like this. I do not understand their surprise. Why greet someone if you do not intend for them to be close to you? Your greetings cannot be brief, silent moments—not in Zanzibar. In fairness to them, they are surprised to learn that they beckoned when they meant to greet. Either way, a momentary wiggle of fingers is clearly not a sufficient hello—they must know this.

Anyway, I have a choice because Mzee Kahawa summons me with a tired gesture once again. My belly does a funny thing and feels dizzyingly empty. It is very much rude to disobey an elder, but I am also too surprised that this elder has noticed me. Stuffing my notepad into a breast pocket under my black *shungi* I rise from the safety of my corner, and I enter the boisterous drama of Jaws Corner.

Since Jaws Corner sits at an intersection of four main streets, it is very common for all people to walk through: Italian and Japanese tourists, local politicians, Catholic Goans, squeaking bicycles, mosque-going boys, and market-going ladies. But still, I feel nervous for being in this space. I am not an elderly man or a brave lady who drinks coffee. I am not a young hair cutter with trendy blue jeans. I am not a fat CUF politician who cheers at the TV and plays checkers. I am not mosque-going or market-going, I am not even squeaking. I am just a girl, much less tall than the coral rock walls all around me and much less brave than the confident, *wazungu* ladies.

When my feet reach Mzee Hanywi Kahawa, my throat murmurs a greeting. To be truthful with you, I am not sure I myself hear it.

The wrinkles at Mzee Kahawa's brow become very deep and it is clear that he has not heard me, so again louder, "*Cheichei, babu.*"

"*Cheichei, mwanangu.*"

I want to say that he smiles, but it is hard to say this truthfully. His eyes smile vaguely, perhaps. It may be that Mzee Kahawa's mouth left its smile in one of those other Zanzibars my mother would tell you of. Anyway, I know that he is pleased to hear my traditional greeting.

As Swahili elders do, he continues by asking me how my mother and father are—

"—*hawajambo*—"

—how it is at home—

"—*hatujambo*—"

—how studies are at school—

"—*mazuri*—"

—how my health is really—

"—*nzuri tu, babu, asante.*"

Then, he asks me what it is which I am doing now. Owh.

"Just…I am sitting."

He groans softly, and I can see the lonely bottom tooth when he says, "Me, I am just sitting, *mwanangu*. Are you doing the same as me?"

I have been caught. The watched one has seen the watcher.

"I draw pictures."

"*Alaa.* Let's see, then."

Disaster has struck.

"Eh…ah, they are not good, *babu* you will not be amused by them."

"Is it?" His droopy eyelids slide upward the slightest distance: this is surprise. Since I know that he has seen and known all there is to see and know, I know that he is being silly. He cannot be surprised.

"Alright, then, child. Greet those at home." He dismisses me.

"Yes, *babu, asante.*"

My feet scurry away from Jaws Corner and past my own corner. I see that in the short time I spent with Mzee Kahawa, a few small children have decided to take up residence on my stoop. This is fine. I am finished with notetaking for now. So, I leave my corner to those children who sit and to the tailor within. I do not return to sit *barazani*.

Instead, my feet take me through the narrow alley beyond them. Above, a house girl cracks a damp bedsheet before hanging it over a balcony to dry in the sun. Her skirt dances in a breeze created by the sheet's motion. Below, the sun has already done its job on the stone street. It is very dry. For that, I am grateful.

Walking through these alleys usually means soggy feet. Puddles collect so easily in old Stonetown. Between slabs of coral rock, rain waters can sit stagnant. Such an old place, Stonetown has probably been built with many fewer people in mind. Now, mangrove poles are tested by the weight of families who live above families underneath even more families. In some places, poles have surrendered and homes have come tumbling down. As if from big, brittle cakes, concrete crumbs scatter across puddles in the street. Where we are living in Kikwajuni most of us live in flat, one-story buildings with metal roofs. There, we have less strained poles, but we are still having plenty of puddles, all the same.

If puddles were shillings, we would all be wealthy enough to live in those marbled floor homes in Chukwani. Our shoes would always be polished like the *mzungu* who runs at Kiwimbi, and our feet would be spotlessly clean. But, puddles are not shillings—they are dirty water. We march through them splashing, *dwa-dwa-dwa*. Those of us without shoes pray for health and those of us with shoes pray for aunties' forgiveness when we step inside.

Anyway, today is a dry day. I have no puddles to consider—or shillings, either. My feet do not preoccupy themselves with finding the shallowest waters because the stone street is nicely clean, shining in the gentle, July sun. Even on dry days, a girl must be a little cautious, though. Stonetown is so narrow and winding.

My feet do quick dances to avoid fish sellers on bicycles '*mia-tano-mia-tanoo*' and tourists in beige hats '*oh-yes-aah*.' They know their way, my feet, and they adjust to interruptions of new visitors. They beat a rhythm on the stones, continuing like this until they reach Haile Selassie Road.

This is where my school is, on this road. Sometimes on maps, you can find names like Creek Road and Benjamin Mkapa Road here on this space. Bwana Usi, our neighbor who has a touch-phone, he has shown me. There is a map on his phone with Benjamin Mkapa written here and nothing at all written in Kikwajuni.

But everyone I know, we call this road Haile Selassie. A very straight and wide road, it reaches the whole way from the old port to the football fields by Kiwimbi. It makes a triangle out of Stonetown in this way. On the edge of that triangle, my school sits behind its gated wall.

The gated wall, it is that same cream color of Mzee Kahawa's *kanzu*. The grand name of our school adorns it, and the suggestion of an outline of two figures rests on one side. These figures have been painted by a group of Form 4 learners whose idea has won a contest this month. Me, I do not think their idea is so wonderful, but yes, it is better than the other ones. Therefore, soon a boy and a girl in the uniform of Haile Selassie will live a blue-and-brown-painted life on our wall.

Beyond the wall, its painted title, and its boy-and-girl-outline, there are some learners. Although, many are absent. Like me, my exams have been written and done since the day before yesterday. I am fortunate. For me, it means that I have two or three days to look carefully at unusual people and take my notes. I relax until Ramadhan begins, and I write.

For others, I suppose it means time to play football or to visit family in *shamba*—the countryside. We have cousins out in *shamba* who grow cassava next to their house. I expect to celebrate the end of Ramadhan with them, but let them come to us and let us all go together on a day out to the beach. This is a nicer plan. Besides, it is what we have done other times. *Shamba*, it is just too far and too hot. Me, I like to be closer to the sea. Here, there are breezes which cool down the hottest days.

Just now, a breeze is swirling around me. Though, today is not a hot day so this one, it is a little bit chilling. A tall palm at the end of Haile Selassie Road shivers in the cool wind, shaking subtly from side to side. This wind is coming from the south, the direction of Kiwimbi. For now, I do not go back to Kiwimbi, though. I stay here by my school.

Through the open gate of Haile Selassie Secondary School, I search for noteworthy people. Today is the last day of writing exams. After these, we have our holiday during the month of fasting. Thus, I see the Form 3 and 4 learners in a ground floor hall, sweating over exam papers. A few white shirts have yellowed around the sweaty hems. One learner has fallen asleep, his hand askew and his face smeared with graphite from blurry exchanges with his own written responses.

Some Form 2 learners are also present and sweating as they swing machetes, trimming tall grasses between the main building and the State University library. The boys have unbuttoned their shirts to let the breeze in and the sweat out. Swinging their machetes is easier that way, too, I suppose—arms unrestricted by tight sleeves.

Overseeing the sweating and the swinging is an instructor of health and environment. He is a short, round man. I have seen him at Kiwimbi doing sit-ups before. I tell you, he is not very good at them, but assuredly he tries. His wife must press him to keep trying. That is his reason for doing something he so clearly does not do happily or well.

None of these people or their behavior is unusual, so I do not reach for my notepad. However, I do find a nice place for sitting. Past the school's wall, there is a small store with soap, phone cards, and fried sweets. Next to this small store, a man is selling oranges and tangerines. Behind this man and his fruits, there is a little stoop. Here is where I sit.

From my stoop, I can view Jamhuri Gardens which lie across the big road from my school. Jamhuri Gardens is a nice place most times. We often go there for birthdays. My little sister—owh, well she is my 'cousin' in English—especially loves the swings and the slides. Learners like to study in the gardens, too, but none are sitting on the grass today. Today, if one does not have an exam to write, then surely she is elsewhere.

Instead, a few young men and women sit there on benches where mosquitoes nibble at ankles. These young adults do not think others know that they are dating, but this is what everyone knows. Even from across the wide road, I can see their cautious hands touch at the fingertips. This is quite an ordinary thing to take place at Jamhuri Gardens.

Therefore, my eyes are drawn to what is unusual now. From behind the man who halves oranges, I am watching young men who gather at the corner of the garden. They sit closely together on the side of the fence which lines the road to Kiswandui, separating the gardens from a muddy path. Young men sitting together—even so closely together—is not special, but I can tell there is something different here.

My bottom scoots to the right to have a better angle, unobstructed by the fruit-selling gentleman's cart. My right hand slips my notepad from my pocket out onto my lap. Its blue cover blends with the blue of my trousers. I like this. It seems to assist in my stealthy work. And, it is time for a new page: Page 23—*the boys who make plans*.

Looking carefully at the boys who make plans is a challenge because they sit across Haile Selassie Road, which is a busy place. Intermittently, passing cars block my view. Also, the road itself is very wide, especially compared to all of the other Stonetown streets. I think this is because it is not really Stonetown anymore, you see. My mother can tell you that her mother would tell you about a time when everything across this road was called Ng'ambo for a reason.

Ng'ambo means 'the other side,' and my mother could tell you that before British men determined to change the land there was no road here. In fact, there was no land here! She will tell you that it was a creek where the ocean sneaked up into Kikwajuni and surrounded Kiswandui, which was a little island then where they put all the sick, sick people to keep away from the healthy ones. Then, the British government saw it fit to fill up the creek, send the ocean back to the beach, and connect the other side with this side.

Now, when we say Ng'ambo it is still the other side but we do not think about creeks or islands. Now, when we say Ng'ambo we are talking about the side without *wazungu*, hotels, or cousins from Punjab. We refer to the side with weddings, football, and cousins from Pemba.

For now, I sit on the side with my notepad and I look at the side with boys who make plans. They are three, and I note this first. The largest one wears a *kofia*. When I say largest know that I mean in his shoulders. None of the young men are large in their bellies. From this, I know that he must prefer maize porridge over *chapati*, which would have made his belly wide like his shoulders. Perhaps he exercises at Kiwimbi, too. In that case, he may eat plenty of *chapati* and even rice since he has an exercise routine. This is how bodies work; they enjoy balance. They forgive your giving them oil for dinner if you give them running and jumping for breakfast.

Anyway, I must focus…*the largest one, he wears a nice* kofia, *folded down in the proper way…his nose is wide and flat…skin darker than mine*…I think he is Pemban…*his family has sent him to Stonetown for school. They trust that an education on Unguja may secure him employment as a teacher*…I wonder if he supports CUF, but I have not seen him in Jaws Corner before. Now, he talks with much seriousness to another young man. He likes to use his hands when he does this. The man he talks to with his words and his hands is a little shorter than him…*This second one has smaller shoulders than the largest man, and he does not wear a* kofia…*He wears a football jersey*—Fly Emirates—*and his head is shaven clean bald*…This smaller, hatless one listens with care to the largest man, and I know this because he has wrinkles above his eyebrows. Ah, perhaps the largest man is also the cleverest man, and this bald one must put in lots of effort in order to understand him. That, too, may be causing these wrinkles.

I note all of these things on Page 23, and it fills up nicely. I can feel my eyes smiling with this achievement. The pen continues onto Page 24. Now, the third boy who makes plans, what is he doing? I cannot see well.

At first, I think he is not listening to the largest, cleverest man at all. Through glasses with wire-thin frames, he looks downward somehow, at his feet or at the ground. His hands, though, they seem to be busying themselves with something. What is he doing, fidgeting and looking downward?

After a long enough break in cars passing, I see what he does. He takes notes—like me! Oh, the boys who make plans look like a right, little committee meeting. This third one is the secretary recording their minutes. The largest one is the chairman. And, the hatless one, I do not know his title.

But, this committee, what is the purpose of their meeting? By their nature, most committee meetings are political. A trio of young men making plans, putting ideas into writing, and doing it while hiding in plain sight: this is very interesting.

The hatless, bald one is the security...Now, I see, yes. Look at the way he glances around corners. He is subtle enough whereby he does not himself look suspect. As you know, however, I am a skilled observer. It is clear to me that his wrinkles are for concern of being seen...*the chairman has a strategy communicated down to him from some superior. He shares it now with the secretary who is going to disseminate the information to others. The security is nervous. He worries that the chairman speaks too boisterously, waving his hands about*...In fact, that one is gripping the largest one by the wrist now and saying something to him.

The secretary puts his notes in a shirt pocket, and the three stand. Brushing dust from their bottoms, the committee seems to have adjourned. Indeed, they move away from their place toward the football fields by the airport road. They do not separate, though, and I wonder if they are only relocating.

Curious, I return my notepad to its pocket and I, too, stand. An opportune moment comes just now when no cars block my crossing, so I calmly traverse the wide road. Good, let me appear calm and typical. The secretive committeemen shall not know that they have an onlooker. But yes, my job is not finished, I think. I think there is more to be learned from watching these scheming boys.

Thus, I follow in their wake as Mr. Chairman leads his committeemen southward toward the airport road. I am a little spy boat which trails a navy warship, undetected. Passersby are the erratic waves, providing my cover. Besides, girls like me, we are not to be suspected. We run errands and fetch things from market. We are not observant investigators, watching carefully and taking notes. Well, most of us, we are not.

The boys who make plans continue onward. Turning left around a corner where the public buses sit, they enter Kikwajuni. The broad-shouldered one and the secretary appear to be disagreeing on something. I resolve to note this once I am no longer mobile. A challenge in the chain of command, perhaps, and this could mean a variety of things.

They carry on, however. They pass the gym, briefly and boisterously greeting a few young men there with smiles and a grasping of hands. Next, *assalaam-aleykum* is exchanged with the elder men who drink their morning coffee. They sit under a Zantel umbrella. Its green color is like avocado, but brighter still, so very green. Contrastingly, the elder men have adorned themselves in simple garments much like Mzee Kahawa's creams and browns. This is typical. It is the young boys who like to wear flashy pinks and oranges.

I tell you, boys in my generation, they are like peacocks. Auntie likes to tease them all for this. Men of her age, and elders like these who sit here, they prefer unremarkable and neutral hues. They see no value in grabbing at attentions. Rather, they admire quiet conformity—a visibly unified community.

The boys who make plans, they fit somewhere between these two traditions. As I have told you, the security is wearing his *Fly Emirates* jersey, but he also has a cleanly shorn head. His comrades are keeping tidy, respectful looks, as well. The chairman is wearing his *kofia* properly. Whereas Mzee Hanywi Kahawa, an icon of time, clumsily tops his head with a floppy flower pot of a hat; here is a young adolescent dressed like an imam in training. This contrast intrigues me.

Finally, the committee seems to arrive at their destination. They perch themselves on a stoop halfway between the gym and Kiwimbi beach. This stoop leads up into an ice cream parlor, but its hefty, iron gate is locked shut. Me, I do not frequent this side of Kikwajuni. Auntie warns us that mainlanders who smoke *bangi* like to mingle over on this side. Do the boys who make plans smoke *bangi*? They certainly do not look like any mainlanders I know.

Suddenly, I am aware that our new location does not provide me the natural cover of passersby. I am at a loss for convenient hiding places, so my feet stop me just where I am, and I sit here on the grassy pebbles between football field and road. I withdraw my notepad, but I pretend to read it at first. If I immediately restart taking notes, they will likely notice my behavior.

The best detectives on the Indian dramas, they wait until the optimal moment for action lest they 'blow their cover.' What a funny phrase, this one. It makes me envision a girl like me hiding behind bedsheet covers on a line to dry. If the covers blow too much in the breeze, then her hiding place is revealed.

Maybe this is where the phrase comes from. Perhaps I am not the first girl to make a habit of hiding and carefully watching. That explains this phrase. For now, like my forebears before me, I must ensure my covers are not blown.

As for the boys who make plans, they do immediately restart their work. The secretary is encouraging the largest one to begin, prodding him with a pen. The bald one, he looks casually about, and within moments he sees me. I train my eyes on the salon behind them. My covers! Have I blown them so quickly?

Then, it seems I am alright. Perhaps the bald one thinks like many do; he thinks that girls like me, we run errands or fetch things from the market. We do not investigate. We do not spy.

Still, I must be cautious because this place is far from any market or errand apart from collecting beach sand with which to scrub cooking pots. Hm, if I am confronted, that is just what I may tell these boys: I am on my way to gather some sand from Kiwimbi, and I have grown tired from the long walk. I am only sitting for a time to breathe. Does a girl not have a right to sit and regain her breath? I think so.

With these newfound, unblown covers, I regain confidence. I can take advantage of the security boy's assumptions about who it is that I am and what it is that I do not do. Slipping the pen into my fingers, my hand begins its work once more on Page 24.

The secretary writes feverishly. His glasses slide toward the tip of his nose… he records everything that the chairman says now…it is the most important part of the plan. I admit, it is hard to tell from a distance what it is that they plan. I must look deeper into their appearance, their behavior, their expressions. As I have noted, most committees concern politics. If a committee meets in secret, then clearly it is not one whereby its members hold views which are acceptable to usual politicians.

They are CUF supporters… This is the reason they maintain such secrecy. Or, are they *Uamsho* supporters, even? I tell you, the difference between the two blurs more and more these days. Owh, I ought to explain for you.

The ruling party—union and island both—they are *Chama cha Mapinduzi*, CCM. They call themselves *cha mapinduzi* because they have been in charge since the revolution. The party who opposes them is the one I have told you about in Jaws Corner, the Civic United Front. CUF, as they are called by their members as well as their enemies, is most popular on Pemba. I often hear this said, anyway. Our neighbor, Usi, has told me that no one on Unguja votes for CUF—they are all Pembans. Maybe it is true. But, I tell you also, I do not think Bwana Usi has ever been to Pemba. Thus, I let you decide, yourself.

Now, *Uamsho*, this is not a party. The word '*uamsho*,' it means waking up, or 'awakening,' I suppose. *Wauamsho* want Zanzibar to be independent from the mainland. They do not support the union. Rather, they think islanders ought to wake up—like we are all dreaming a bad dream in bed.

They believe that it is time to get out of this bed politicians have made for us. I know their name, because I have heard Usi say it to Auntie. When he says it, Auntie becomes upset and makes him stop speaking. I think that *Uamsho* must be dangerous. Why else would Auntie disallow it in our house? They must be doing something naughty, something much too bold.

It is confusing, though. You see, because I have also heard Auntie say that we on Unguja would be better as our own country—we would be richer and happier without the mainland—back to the ways of her mother's time when the islands were closer to Omani sultans than African presidents; when there was no rubbish on the streets and when schools were efficient places with beautiful English, she says.

Auntie seems to like what *Uamsho* likes, but she does not seem to like *Uamsho*. Perhaps it is the English. I do not think *wauamsho* care for beautiful English. I do not think that is necessarily one of their priorities. I surmise that 'awakening' puts English skills at a lower priority than political independence.

The boys who make plans, they are wauamsho…This is why they huddle privately and hold an air of bold, naughty schemes. The feeling is just like the times Usi speaks to Auntie, and she hushes up his gossip. Auntie would not sit as I do and contemplate these boys who make plans. She would approach them and end their meeting with a scolding. Me, I am not Auntie.

The chairman's parents have sent word to him through his uncle in Bububu… they have asked him to assist Uamsho…*they have said he makes them proud,* they hope he can free Zanzibar from the unjust union…this exceeds their greatest hopes for him, and they have faith in his ability. He is a good speaker. He inspires his peers.

The secretary, he admires his friend, Yusuf, the chairman…Yusuf has persuaded him to help…this one, he is a fast writer…his parents say he has been reading and writing since a very young age…they credit his madrassa teacher, masha'allah.

The security, he is the neighbor of the secretary, Gharib…he is not clever, but he is intimidating…he is always the first player to be thrown out of football matches because he tackles or throws fists at some other poor boy…His eyes, they are stern like the wild animals I have seen on television.

In fact, he is reminding me now of the hippos I have seen on a certain channel. On that one, English men and ladies narrate the lives of mainland animals. His eyes look about in the way that the hippos' eyes do. Everything annoys them. The birds, the people, the trees, and the air itself—they are all suspect and aggravating things to hippos.

As my eyes carefully watch the boys who make plans, I wonder if it becomes clearer that I am not here just to sit and regain breath. Probably, it has become too clear. Even as the security seems to have accepted my presence, he is beginning to target me with more and more hippo-eyed glances.

What is it that the English lady says about hippos on TV? Owh, they are not fast in water as many think, no. They are much faster on land. This is surprising knowledge, since they are not clever and so very round.

As the security boy holds his stare, I am wondering if he is faster on land or in water. Regardless, me, I am not quick in either setting, myself. My fingers stray away from writing. I cannot help it: my eyes meet his own and meekly return his fierce gaze. He spits a word at the chairman boy, whom I have dubbed Yusuf. Yusuf nods vaguely. Then, the security starts to cross the street.

I tell you, if I must endure confrontation each time I carefully watch and take notes, well, soon I may just stop altogether. *Mungu wangu, jamani.*

He reaches me. My eyes have pretended to find fascination in a palm tree to their right.

"You! What are you doing?"

My chin turns around in insincere surprise.

"Hm?"

His hippo eyes burn with an unkind fire.

"Little know-it-all girl! Why are you sitting here?"

"Just…just, I am regaining my breath," I stammer, vaguely remembering a plan, "I am on my way to gather sand for washing, I—"

He laughs an ugly laugh. That, it is a bully's laugh. It calls me foolish and hushes up my words.

"You think you are clever. You are not, *weye*. Get away from here! This is our place here!"

Without meaning to, I suck my teeth in disdain. Their 'place,' oh! He is very rude, this one. And, he only confirms all of my observations. They are indeed a sneaky, scheming group, these boys who make unacceptable plans.

"What are *you* doing?" I snap before I can stop myself.

His hippo eyes widen. They transform into lion eyes, and he unleashes his claws—an angry hunter. I am the ambushed gazelle with all of her covers quite completely blown.

With predatory strength, he shoves me in the shoulder. I fall backward into the brush. My lungs let out a shout as stiff stems stab me in the back and the bottom. Oh! This one! I hope he and his friends get a real beating. Who do they think they are!

My notepad has fallen into the weeds, and my headscarf comes nearly undone. Responsive fingers do quick work to gather both up before this boy can notice either item askew. Without headscarf or notepad alike, I feel naked: a naked gazelle, maimed in the brush and exposed before a reckless predator.

Gathering myself together I lift up, and feeling more controlled—or less brave—my voice keeps silent now. I simply stomp my right foot, and stalk off. The boy is nodding victoriously while I turn away from him and his comrades. This time, the prey has survived. I hope never again to meet these predators.

Even so, my heart beats too strongly in my chest. I know that I am safe again as I walk along the football field, but my heart has not caught up to my brain. It pounds *pa-pa, pa-pa-pa* like I have run a race.

My feet stomp past the elders under their very green umbrella while my hand is cradling its precious notepad in my pocket. I do not greet anyone, lest they ask me what I do or where it is that I go. Let me be the one to know. I grow tired of encounters when me, I just want to observe. I want to be a good detective.

Just behind one of the elder's chairs, I perceive a whisper of movement. *Pa-pa-pa, pa-pa-pa*, my heart runs a race in my chest. As I pass him and his sand-speckled chair I do not see anything there. For a moment, I have thought a—but, no—just, my eyes are confused. It is nothing.

My heart is slowly finding its regular rhythm *pa, pa-pa*. But my feet, where is it that you take me now? Khadija writes her final exam at school. Do we go and see if she has finished? Despite uninvited interruptions, notetaking has gone well this morning. I have learned much about Mzee Kahawa and the boys who make plans. I have largely succeeded in carefully watching like the detectives on the Indian dramas. If someone asks me to tell them about the ones I watch, I can tell them many good, accurate things, yes.

Thus, I persuade my feet to take us back to Jamhuri Gardens. There, families and young couples can be found—even at this time in the morning. I wish to keep my observations going.

I expect to find learners like me, liberated from exams but aimless before Ramadhan's beginning. I expect to spy discreet couples, who cannot meet like this during the Holy Month, secretly touching fingertips. Also, I expect to find the youngest children playing on slides and swings. Plastic crocodiles display menacing teeth, but Stonetown children laugh and pay them no mind. A ceramic giraffe stands tall over the playground. Now that I am older, she looks so feeble to me, but once again I do not imagine that it makes a difference to the ones so young. They delight in her presence. They do not analyze the frailness of her stature.

These young ones accompanied by big sisters or aunties, they play now before dusk when mosquitoes wake up. They play now, too, before Ramadhan when daytime has a very different feeling. From sunrise until sundown during Ramadhan, Stonetown transforms into a quiet and sleepy place. Cafes close.

Only the market stays open. An energy like a dream descends because stomachs are empty and spirits are full.

During this time, they say that spirits are particularly active. Auntie tells me that in the days before Ramadhan, energies change because of preparation. I have seen it, so I believe her. There are many weddings just before the Holy Month. This means late-night parties where brides are surrounded in advice and jubilation. It can mean imbibing—cloves or alcohol—the latter more *haram* than the former. It means excitement.

On the other hand, some begin to fast early. For some, it is for knowing that they must travel and will be unable to fast during that time. So, they compensate now. For others, it is just preparation. They train their bodies now to make fasting during the Holy Month more manageable. They wish to focus on introspection and charity, and less on hunger pains. It makes for a solemn atmosphere.

Me, I have fasted. Though, I have not fasted all the way through. I eat breakfast just after sunrise, or sometimes I have a snack in the afternoon. I am young, so it is forgiven. Soon, though, I am expected to grow up and to participate with full intention.

Anyway, this excitement and this solemnity make for a spiritual mixture. Perhaps this is the reason for the spirits' awakening. Auntie and my mother, they might say so. I am unsure, but I am inclined to believe them. I tell you, in these days just before Ramadhan, I have seen women fall to the ground in a panic. They flail and shriek like wild animals. My mother, she may say that it is a possession. Auntie, she says that is precisely what it is. They attribute this to the spirits' liveliness.

Owh, but I do not mean to bore you with such things. Surely, you do not believe in spirits or possessions.

My feet continue through Jamhuri Gardens. Let us see what I can find here.

WEDNESDAY AFTERNOON

MY FEET APPROACH AN OPENING in the chain fence around Jamhuri. On the other side, two ladies are sitting on a bare spot beside a slide. That one, I think it is quite old. Its frame is a bit warped and its blue paint is flaking like some animal has taken to scratching it. Disregarding its flaky, oceanic decoration, I consider the ladies instead.

One of them, she wears her hair wrapped up in a pretty scarf. Its color reminds me of honey. She holds her companion's hand, and wrapped around that one I see that her nails are polished to match the scarf. I like this. The other, she wears *niqab*; black fabric covering her up from head to toe. Only her eyes are visible through a small slit in the graying black mask tied behind her head by a thin string. In appearance, this duo is not unlike Auntie and Mother.

This year for Ramadhan, Auntie has insisted that I fast from *alfajiri* to *ishaa* like a proper Muslim lady—sunrise to sundown. She says I am plenty old enough and I should have been fasting this way already. She asserts that my afternoon snacks are less *halali* now that I am nearly a young woman. Maybe she is right. And, I think I can do it.

However, I resist her anyway because I know that if I accept so easily then she may try to suggest other things, too. Next, she may tell me that I wear the wrong headscarf, and after that, she may tell me that I must wear *niqab* during fasting. You know, after that she may tell me that I ought to wear *niqab* all the time, like this lady here in the Gardens! Oh no, I do not think so. This is why I resist now, you see.

Auntie, she is that way. During the Holy Month, she likes to dress in *niqabu*, covering all but her eyes. When she goes to market or to formal events, she wears black from head to toe. Sometimes, she wears black gloves which extend to her elbows. Though they are sisters, Auntie and my mother, it is as if they might have had different upbringings entirely.

While Auntie would disappear into blackness and take me with her, my mother would wear pink and yellow colors. During Ramadhan, my mother may lighten her words and her deeds but she would not darken her fabrics.

Even so, resisting Auntie aloud is a difficult thing. I am a girl. Girls do not get to tell elders what is right. Elders tell us what is right and what ought to be done. Obviously, that is the way things are. If I wish to contradict my elders, then I must have a reason as clear and strong as diamonds.

I tell you, I have said no to Auntie before. It is not often successful. From this, I have learned that when I say no, I must say it very strategically. Each word must be selected as thoughtfully as a dance step, weaving in and out of acceptability lest I place a foot wrong and get a beating. I suppose it is like dancing for a crocodile. If my fancy feet can distract Mama Crocodile, then I might survive. If I step wrong, then her teeth—or her belt, really—meet my bottom. I have met those teeth before. They make for days of very uncomfortable sitting. Thus, how to dance this time? What steps—what words—are just right?

In Swahili, we have many ways to say things without saying them so directly. Once one says exactly the words she means to say she often finds that those words betray her and take up a violent, unpredictable life of their own. So, as much as possible it is better to communicate without taking risk of empowering dangerous words.

One of these ways is through *methali*. You might call these proverbs. Proverbs are tried and tested words which are known not to betray their speakers. Anyone who hears a *methali* can understand what she wishes, but the speaker can never be accused of meaning ill. This is how we regain control of tricky words and hide our meaning within them.

There is one proverb which says '*If you are given a span, do not take the whole measure*.' It would be good to tell my auntie this *methali*. Then, she might know that by fasting I am giving her a span, but I do not give her the whole measure. Still, Mama Crocodile cannot bare her teeth at me for saying so—they are not my words, but the *methali*.

Well, I suppose she is always my elder. She can bare her teeth whenever she likes. Still, it is worth a try. It is better than not resisting at all, and allowing her to drag me into black depths of billowy fabrics. Indeed, a gnashing of teeth is not so bad. Maybe I get one beating, but the topic goes forgotten. One beating for less demands: that deal is not so bad.

In fact, this gives me a very good idea. I redirect my feet toward Darajani. The Gardens, they may wait for another time. In Darajani, I can find the fabric vendors, and perhaps they have a *kanga* with this proverb printed on it. I can wear it, Auntie may see it, and she will know my feelings. I could even wear this *kanga* at home while I am fasting so she may see it every day—I could even wear it in *niqab* style, hee! I fast, Auntie, yes, but you will not have the whole measure!

This idea delights me so. My lips cautiously curve into a smile, which my hand hides until it has finished so that nobody may think I am full of foolish thoughts. If I am full of mischievous thinking, let me alone be the one to know it.

My feet guide me past the *daladala*, public buses, on the Ng'ambo side of Haile Selassie. They skip over a gap in the pavement where a bit of mud has collected. Then, they navigate toward shade. Afternoon sun has arrived, and it is much meaner than its morning counterpart. No worries to be had, though, for the shade is cool refuge.

This side of the road is a messy place. When I say messy, I mean in several ways. First, a plethora of plastic, orange rinds, and scraps of fabrics have collected here on the pavement. The market lies just north and across the street, so banana peels and discarded apple cores easily end up here, scattered on the ground. They are accompanied by slimy mango seeds and tangerine peels, dried up by the sun. The *daladala* do not mind the forlorn fruit. They drive right over them, occasionally sending a mango seed rolling into the road.

The second kind of messy here is the bustle of people themselves. Everyone finds their way between everyone else. *Daladala* buses do not wait to find their way—they make it. Shouting, whistling, honking, and chattering permeate this space. Corn and cassava crackle on charcoal grills manned by men with parasols. Boys beg their mothers to buy them some. Ladies from *shamba* hoist buckets of cooking oil into buses. Beside those ones, fishermen shove buckets of freshly dead octopus. Mamas rest their sleepy babies on the laps of neighbors, carefully avoiding the chickens who perch on the laps of others.

Conductors shout like auctioneers, only their items for sale are destinations. I have never understood this since each *daladala* is adorned with its destination in clear, black letters. Owh, I suppose not everyone can read. Some have no choice but to listen.

All the mess is multiplied, too, because Ramadhan approaches. With two—is it three?—days left to us, some rush to prepare ingredients. Some rush out to be in *shamba* with families. Other rush in from Dar es Salaam, Dubai, or Europe. Movement, noises, activities of all kinds are messier until the start of the Holy Month when all these things go still; when each breath becomes a prayer and each meal a candlelit feast.

Fortunately, I do not need to enter the mess. Just, I am passing by on the pavement. Rubbish and people spill over onto this sidewalk. Here with cars coming and going, people walking, rubbish collecting, there is no room for trees. I cannot hide from the mean afternoon sun. But, it does not last long.

Now, on my right side there lies Vikokotoni and its clothing. Vikokotoni is a labyrinth, and I do not enter it. The only times I have ever gone in have been accompanied by my mother or by Auntie. Those visits have been for finding especially nice dresses. We cannot usually afford those ones, our family.

Another landmark nestled in Vikokotoni's side of Haile Selassie Road is Ijumaa Mosque. That one, it is busy just like the markets and winding alleys all around it. Of course, every mosque is most lively on Fridays at *adhuhuri* prayer. Still, Ijumaa Mosque is especially alive for Friday prayer. Ijumaa is special because it keeps a large, nicely paved outdoor space. Many mosques in crowded Stonetown have no room at all for outdoor prayer.

In fact, I will tell you one more thing, too. Bwana Usi has told me that Ijumaa Mosque, it has many *wauamsho* in its attendance. He himself, he regularly attends Sheikh Kareem. That one is a grand one very near Auntie's house with cream-colored walls and beautifully smooth steps. But even Sheikh Kareem is not having the outdoor space like Ijumaa, and since men pray there on the patio like that, Bwana Usi says that he has recognized *Uamsho* members there. I am not sure why this is important, but anything that provokes Auntie's hissing disdain is something intriguing to me.

South of Ijumaa Mosque, I am standing at the entrance of Vikokotoni's labyrinthine shops. Here, leather shoes are arranged on waist-high displays. Beside those, fluffy bath towels are on sale today. Do not ask me why anyone would want a thick bath towel when she can buy a *kanga*. After washing a *kanga*, it dries on the line in just an hour of sunlight. Those expensive towels which Westerners prefer, I tell you, they are still damp after a whole day in the sun. Or, they quickly become coarse and unpleasant to touch. Give me thin, cotton *kanga* any day, thank you very much indeed.

Though I stand a moment in Vikokotoni's entrance with its eccentric wares, I do not enter. Rather, this marks the place where I must cross Haile Selassie Road. Opposite, lies Darajani.

Like Kiwimbi, Darajani is a good place to meet people. However, it is not the same thing. I mean to say, at Kiwimbi a girl can see far away down the open spaces between tree line and shoreline. Therefore, it is convenient for meeting. People can find each other there.

In the market at Darajani, a girl cannot see past two feet to any side of herself. But, everyone comes here. Therefore, it is convenient for meeting. People can find each other here, whether they have intended to or not. While the Ng'ambo side of Haile Selassie is a busy mess, Darajani Market is a messy business.

Like Jaws Corner, Darajani is also a dramatic place. Fish sellers shout, customers bargain, and bicycle brakes strain to breaking point. But, here in Darajani market I am not having my own corner. I am not feeling so much like 'just a girl.' Jaws Corner is a space for certain types of people. Darajani is a space for anyone.

Granted, both places have coffee. So, when we gather around coffee as a bean we have more freedom than when it is liquid. Is it? When it becomes liquid, then men and brave *wazungu* ladies take ownership. When it is a bean next to lemongrass, next to saffron and mangoes, sardines, ground beef, peanuts, and eggplants; then it is publicly owned. This is possible, but what a strange rule. They have not taught us this rule at Haile Selassie Secondary School.

Darajani Market is actually divided into several markets, all hugging Haile Selassie Road. Our school is not close enough to the market for the sounds of children to be heard, but the clamorous commotion of cars is ever present here.

A fish market ends where a meat market begins, and the spice market is sheltered under vibrantly orange-colored canopies. Under these canopies, spices are arranged in tight, plastic packages. They have multilingual labels in cheerful fonts. Me, I have never asked for their prices. Tourists are drawn to these spices and to the persuasive men with floppy hats and *marasta* hair who sell them. This covered portion of the market is good for fruit, though. I have seen many ladies from the hotels buying bananas and papaya here in bulk.

Farther down, other shops present phones, *kofia*, soaps, and various many things. Date sellers line another street. In December, those date sellers offer chunks of jackfruit, too; dipping fingertips into oil between cuts to better handle the sticky, sappy fruit which they wrap in scraps of *Nipashe* and *Zanzibar Leo*.

Other vendors pour peanuts, sorghum, lentils, into woven baskets. The baskets rest on scales. After determining the price by kilo, the goods are scooped into stiff paper bags. We do not use plastic bags here on Unguja. Auntie says that plastic bags ruin nature and hurt animals, so this is why we have banned them. Me, I am not sure what animals she is referring to. She must mean fish in the sea. In Stonetown, there are just crows. But, they are naughty, mean birds. Let those ones be hurt, I say, it is no pity.

Just now, a crow lands clumsily next to me. For a moment, a vendor steps away from his wares and the bird takes advantage of it. Feathers a color like dingy socks ruffle and toes as sharp as little knives sink into a kingfish head. A neighboring vendor startles and shouts the bird away, but not before the crow shouts back—*kraa*! *kra aa*! These Stonetown crows, they are malicious creatures.

A sharp, metallic screech fills the silence left by the angry bird. I see tired men are pushing creaky bicycles, coconuts hanging from both sides in burlap bundles bigger than Bwana Usi's belly. Warped tires sway under the weight. Whenever a bundle pulls the contraption's momentum just too much and the men must readjust, wheels unleash the scraping, squealing screech.

While watching the pained bicycles turn and wail under their load, I feel a moistness on my feet. Oh! They have stepped right into some muddle of dark liquid. Bicycle tires and feet alike, they manage somehow to find wet pavement no matter the day's weather. Even when it is not raining, I tell you, Darajani Market seems always to be anointed with some sort of trickling liquid. Sometimes it is water. Other times, it is blood from a shark as men cleave it into market-worthy portions. Still other times, it is an unidentifiable mixture: rains overflow, blending sewers and waters and the fishermen's catches.

These sloppy streams are like the veins and arteries which link each part of the market. They flow out and away from the meat-market-heart and into its spice-market-limbs. Unlike arteries, I do not think they give life or warmth to the parts they touch. Quite the opposite, they are damp and undesirable.

If anything brings life by its movement here, it is the people. They are also like streams—like pumping arteries. Ladies in *baibui* pick up mangoes and take them to families as far as Bububu or Tomondo. Young men race about, moving money from one hand into another. You know, perhaps it is indeed the people who are the market's pumping blood. Then, what of those damp trickles? I say, perhaps they are just what they are—the shit!…Forgive me, my mind wanders.

For now, I am not concerned with any of these. My feet take me to the alleyways behind the spice market. Past the Indian pharmacy and the air-conditioned grocery store, past the Arab *babu* who sells biscuits, over a little wall: this is where the fabric vendors organize.

Here, wares are displayed on all available surfaces. I run two fingers along the flaking paint of stoops covered in meters of wax prints. Where the stoops end, feeble tables are set up in narrow side-streets. Scarves, harem pants, and Maasai cloths hang from hooks which hang from ropes tied to windowsills. Beside each exhibit, vendors are standing prepared for passersby, hoping to catch a curious eye. These men are masters of *kanga* and *kitenge*. If you do not know these words already, you must learn them.

Kitenge are sturdy lengths of stiff cotton. They make good shirts and dresses. Well, as long as they are taken to good tailors, they do. The gentleman over in my section of Jaws Corner, he is a good one. Here on my left side, a young woman with a fancy clip on her headscarf is flicking through a pile of waxprint *kitenge*. She is hunting for something. Perhaps she looks for a fabric to match the fierce pinkness of her fancy clip.

Me, I do not have money enough for waxprint *kitenge* or fancy clips. My pocket keeps barely over 2,000 shillings, which Auntie has given me to hold. She has given me her permission to buy snacks with expectations that I share them with my brother. But, these couple thousand shillings might be enough for one *doti*.

Kanga come in pairs. We call these pairs *doti*. They are the perfect gift. Each *doti* comprises two identical cloths, and we cut them down the middle after purchase. This way, a woman can have a full outift—matching scarf and skirt—from one purchase.

Kanga, they are the perfect gift, but they are versatile. They are also the perfect headscarf, weapon, and washrag. *Kanga* are very multifunctional, you see. I think this is because each *doti* comes with a name nestled in the center of its design—owh, caption is a better word for you, perhaps. This caption determines the best function for each *kanga*.

For example, some read "God bless your wedding," and these are perfect gifts. Others read "May I walk with peace," and those are the perfect headscarves. Others still, they read "Do not talk about things which do not belong to you," and those are the best weapons. Finally, some read "Blussings for your famree," and these are the best washrags.

One must always check the caption before purchasing a *kanga*. If one does not, she risks giving the best washrag as a gift or the best weapon as a headscarf. A cloth with beautiful, golden mangoes depicted inside a pleasant, zig-zag border can read such nasty things. Just the same, a bland, white *kanga* with black spots might humbly ask for the greatest of God's love. A girl can get lost in colors and patterns, but the captions are the identity of the thing, I promise you. So, it is the captions I study when I arrive inside my favorite store.

I like this store for a few reasons. One, there are ladies who work here, and it seems right to me that ladies who are the ones wearing *kanga* should be the ones selling the *kanga*. Two, this store has an entrance and an interior whereas others are outdoor, makeshift spaces. I feel safer up these steps and inside a doorway. Three, there are simply more *kanga* here. More *doti* means more chances to find the good caption.

I am ready with the desired one, and I stand with my chin forward. I present myself confidently: a serious girl. I wait.

I wait more. Though I stand tall, the ladies are not seeing me.

"Sorry." I wait. "Sorry, sister?"

"Mmh," a lady acknowledges that she has heard me, but she is busy on her big, touch-phone. Oh, how rude. My lips turn inward a little and suck at my teeth, but I wait.

"Auntie."

"Owh," she looks up from the screen.

"I am looking for a *kanga*."

"Yes," her bored eyes show me that my statement is perfectly predictable.

"Mmh?"

Her eyes return to her phone, held in a hand with elegant henna designs. I wonder if she is getting married, but I do not inquire. Just behind her, I do notice a blue and yellow *kanga* which is very pretty. Its border is lined in thin, yellow stripes. In the middle field, an image of a boat sails on deep, blue seas. The caption is a good one, too. It reads MCHUNGULIA BAHARI SI MSAFIRI; 'the one who only looks at the sea is not a sailor.'

This is nice, but for now it is not the one I need.

"If you are given a span, do not take the whole measure," I recite. "This is the name of the *kanga* I want."

She does not look away from the touch-screen. Oh! Now, she is very rude.

"Auntie—"

"My child, listen to me, have you heard about that thing?"

This is a way Swahili people like to discuss the news. First, they engage you with a question, but I tell you that you do not need to reply. They intend to tell you. And, she does now.

"My child, the news is not good." Her heads tilts toward one shoulder and slowly, somberly shakes. "An accident has happened—a boat accident. It was a ferry boat—a boat with too many people. They are saying that it sank near Chumbe, and they are pulling passengers from the water. Some passengers are not alive, my child."

I have forgotten my clever caption now. It does not seem as clever.

I utter, "*Mungu wangu.*" My God.

"*Inna-lillahi wa inna illahi raj'un*," she solemnly replies; *We belong to God and to Him we shall return.*

Another lady approaches and asks quietly, "You need a *kanga*?"

My lips turn downward to show her my change in priority, no. My feet descend the steps back to the market street. They leave the *kanga* ladies behind as they guide me once more toward a place. Without instructing them, they are taking me back to the place where we sit sometimes by the track at Kiwimbi.

My feet take me recklessly through the trickles of market liquids. A disgruntled crow shuffles to avoid me. I cannot hear him. I cannot hear the fish sellers' shouts or the commotion of cars on Haile Selassie, either. My feet guide me zombie-like to the Ng'ambo side of the road. I know why they are taking me to Kiwimbi, so I do not question them and I do not stop them.

My feet and I go to Kiwimbi, you see, because this kind of thing—this bad news, this accident—has happened before. Before, the fields by Kiwimbi are where all of those passengers arrive. I mean the ones pulled from the water. Then, all the people who are able come to Kiwimbi and they look at the passengers. They do this to be certain that the cold faces do not match the faces of their loved ones.

It is not a good thing, this. There is no good result. If one sees the cold face of her missing kin, her heart breaks, her throat lets loose a wailing cry, and she herself feels very cold indeed. If one does not find the cold face of her missing kin, she still fills with cold dread until the next day or the next when finally she might reunite with her living kin and together they feel warmth again.

So, you see, looking at these passengers, one can only feel cold. One may wail with sorrow or tremble until the next day or even the next. There is no good result either way.

Knowing this, my feet take me to Kiwimbi.

WEDNESDAY EVENING

MY FEET CONTINUE PAST KIKWAJUNI'S gym. They do not proceed to the place where the boys who make plans have met earlier today. Rather, they take a turn and cut directly across the field in order to most quickly reach the water. They continue like this until they reach the same driftwood bench they know from their encounter with the mzungu who runs.

Similar to yesterday's encounter, the sun is low on the water—as low as it may go without being fully swallowed up by waves. The sand beneath my feet is cool and dense. This is the way sand becomes on July evenings on Unguja. The tall, tall palms and the short, fat baobabs wiggle in the breeze. Just like any usual evening, I may sit here between the netball goals and the sandy track. The sun, the weather, and the place—they are just like yesterday. Kiwimbi is also similarly busy with activity.

However, this evening is not busy with jogging, jumping, and running. No one is departing the beach in direction of mosques for *magharibi* prayer. Instead, people are slowly arriving at the beach from town and the airport road. No teams practice capoeira kicks and lunges, focusing breaths between bursts of movement.

Instead, teams of men wearing solemn faces are carrying heavy cargo. These small groups heave loads wrapped up in whatever is available: blankets, *kanga*, tarps. Each one is carried by two or three men, their arms bent at the elbow and straining with unusual weight.

As unusual things are the best for note-taking, my hand withdraws my trusted notepad. Turning to Page 25, I do not put much thought into a heading because clever thoughts are hard to form.

There is so much activity, you see, that I suppose I am distracted. I write simply: *ferry accident—Kiwimbi*. The pen hesitates at the second line while my eyes witness many things. It is not clear which unusual thing should be transferred to writing first.

The entire scene is of course unusual. Kiwimbi, as you know, regularly hosts dozens of people who exercise at this time. Young men use tires for jumping and sit-ups. They balance their bottoms on the half-buried tire while other boys run alongside the water. Ladies jog together in matching yellow-and-green shirts emblazoned with Mr. Barack Obama's smiling face. Capoeira teams move together as if they are fighting, but they are not. In fact, each kick is placed with intention and no one truly gets hurt. It is like a dance.

Typically, the only thing which changes about Kiwimbi from day to day is the tide. Sometimes the water is too high, and those who run cannot exercise on the beach anymore. Other times, the tide is so very low that those who do sit-ups might even do them down on salty, uncovered rocks next to surprised, little crabs who scurry away. For me, I do not like to go on those rocks—they are sharp and slippery. It is a bad combination, sharp and slippery.

On this evening, none of those people are here. None of those activities are happening. No young men jumping, running, or doing sit-ups. No ladies. No teams. No, even the crows are quiet. They know something is unusual tonight.

In fact, a truck full of electric bulbs, wires, and microphones has arrived. It departs the airport road and wobbles through the sand. After halting a few meters to my left, a team of reporters descends with their ropey instruments and hurriedly begins screwing metallic things together. I note that this is the first time a driver has actually sped off the road and right onto the sand, fulfilling that exciting fear of ours.

However, the fear which I am feeling because of it is unexpected. When the hairs on our arms have risen before, it has been for braving the risk of sitting in harm's way. Now, my little hairs feel no accomplishment for being brave about risks. The skin beneath them prickles with anticipation. Those hairs stand straight up in fear of a wicked thing.

There are no people exercising. Yet, much lifting, carrying, and straining of muscles occurs. Though, it is a different sight. It is a very different feeling. When the capoeira teams dance-fight, their breaths are deep and rhythmic.

With each swing of a foot, the dancer exhales firmly. The moments between movements allow for quick, deep inhalations. Today, the teams of men who are carrying wrapped things are not breathing like that.

These men are not inhaling between strategic movements. They are not exhaling rhythmically like dancers. They force breaths sporadically when it is that they remember to do so.

Whereby inhaling gives strength to the dance-fighters and the joggers, these men seem to be feeling quiet pain each time their chests fill with air. I observe this on their faces. It is in their eyes and their chins. Their eyes are having no spirit behind them—only determined duty. Their chins tense and tremble from clenching teeth. I think they are moving like this because of what it is that they carry.

Perhaps it is obvious. I can tell you in case it is not. These heavy loads wrapped in haphazard cloth, they are the most unusual thing on the beach tonight. They are the bodies of the ones who have sunk with the ferry boat.

The men are arranging them in rows under tents, and soon people will come to see if their faces match kin. The people who arrive from town and the airport road, this is why they have come. It is a twisted setting, like a terrible market where shoppers leave with less wealth but instead of gaining spices or fabrics from the transaction they are gaining sorrow and pain.

Many thoughts are traversing my mind, but my pen remains where it has been, stuck at the beginning of the second line under my minimal title. The painful breathing discomforts me, and seeing the cold bodies has frozen my own. The crew of news reporters feels invasive, so I move a little farther away from that place. Normally, unusual things fill me up with intrigue and guide my pen across page after page in my notepad. But now, I do not feel this way.

Instead of intrigue, I am filled up with discomfort. My breaths feel shallow, but there is nothing I can do to change it. My shoulders, they tense. In fact, it is like a presence has arrived and conspires to push on them. This presence digs into my neck and shoulders. Have you ever felt that something unfamiliar has crept up close to you, just behind your ear? This is the feeling. It becomes heavier and heavier. It is the type of feeling that seeks to destroy you if you dare to tell anyone about it. It is unnatural. Just, you must carry on and ignore all the darkest whispers and wonders which fill you up with dread.

My hand is gripping my pen so firmly that I realize it is paining me. I release it, and it happens to fall down into the dense sand. Recollecting it, I brush off the brown sands and hope that it can still write properly. Recollecting myself, I stand and commit to approaching the busy tents. Perhaps if I see these weary people closer up, I can carefully look at them and I may share with you what is interesting and unusual this evening. Perhaps if I keep moving, my shoulders might loosen and I might regain my breath.

After a few steps forward, a lady nearly collides with me from behind. She walks much more quickly than me, but when the hem of her *baibui* catches on my notepad she turns to see what is the matter. Our eyes meet for a moment. I cannot see anything but her eyes since she wears *niqab*, but this is enough.

I tell you, her eyes pierce me with such panic. They are not wide like a child's eyes become when startled. Rather, they are wide like a cat who is hunting. Then, they do not have confidence like a cat who is hunting—not at all! Perhaps the best way to explain these lady's eyes to you is to say that they are like a hunting cat who has been kicked in the side. Even though she is hurt badly, she is hungry and must go on. These are determined eyes—full of confusion and fear—but determined. Then, as suddenly as she has appeared, she is gone toward the nearest tent full of bodies arranged by diligent men.

As she goes, my fingers remind me that they hold a pen. I have much to write about the lady whose eyes display a hunting, startled fear. Perhaps you have seen eyes like these before, but to me they are very unusual.

But, I cannot.

Ordinarily, as you know, this is the moment when I am able to tell much about a person—like the police who investigate a scene and make notes. I am good at carefully looking and knowing these things. But now, I just cannot.

This lady with fearful eyes lies somewhere beyond my understanding. I am not sure of her story, and to be honest with you, it does not feel right to make guesses. The heavy darkness on my shoulders whispers in my ears that I am too small to understand her. It pinches the back of my neck and tells me that I do not even understand myself.

Perhaps that is so. But, I cannot stand here. More ladies rush around me, and I am blocking their way. Acknowledging my fingers gratefully for their patience, I squeeze the pen, but I do not commit any words to writing. Instead, I continue forward.

As my feet cross the threshold of a tent, all of my senses activate. First, my skin is feeling cold and damp as sand sticks to my toes in small clumps. The sand must be wet from the teams of men and their cargoes which have come out from the sea. Then, I am hearing pieces of hushed voices. *Mama no— it is not good—this one here—call her now—go get your brother—inshaallah, inshaallah.* Anxiety in these words infects me. I shiver, not from the cold, but from the emotion. The presence is growing heavier still on my shoulders. I want someone to speak to me, though my mouth is clamped shut. I fear if I open it, my heart will explode. I do not want to carry this feeling alone, but to share it might kill me.

Also, there is a smell here. In addition to the briny ocean smell, my nose fills with an odor I have not experienced before. I tell you, and forgive me for this is not pleasant, it is like my brother's musky pillowcase before a good washing combined with the public toilets at school: only the worst of human smells—salt, sweat, and defecation. This scent fills my nose and seeps into my mouth. I can taste it in some way, and I gag. It takes me a moment to recompose myself. Finally, I allow my eyes to gaze downward and I see what there is to see.

Arranged in rows, clammy faces look upward from stiff bodies. Most eyes have been shut, but this seeing death in a fellow human, oh, it is not easy. I take my time in clipping my pen onto my notepad and placing it in an interior pocket, beneath my *shungi*. I allow this moment to expand for as long as it likes, so long as my body is busy with anything other than smelling that scent and seeing those faces. I admit that the many unusual characteristics of this night are not for notetaking. I put the notepad away, and I forget about Page 25. It is not important anymore. The dark weight on my shoulders tells me that it is not important anymore.

Try as I might, I cannot turn a moment into an eternity. After the notepad is away, I am witnessing death wrapped in wet cloth on grim faces. The sound of uneven, forced breathing returns to my ears, too. Each minute, the teams of men bring another unfortunate passenger onto Kiwimbi.

My feet manage to shuffle forward. I agree with their intent. Let us just go home now. Respectfully, they move slowly and out of the way of the dutiful men. However, my eyes cannot turn away from each body lined up on the ground. I see a child of my age. Perhaps she is here after never having learned to swim. The swollen legs of a woman are exposed, but I dare not touch her garments. I see an old man with frail arms. Perhaps he is here despite knowing how to swim. He is simply too old to have lasting strength. Oh, he reminds me of Mzee Kahawa. Then, I see another.

This cold face looks at me, and I feel that I know it. This damp, brown face is a lady's face. The headscarf she has worn is askew, wrapped awkwardly around her neck and shoulders. Her hair is naked for all to see in this wretched, public space. Men, boys, reporters, strangers, they are all here. And, there is her soggy hair, naked in the night. I want to fix her scarf for her. I want to cover her, and return to her her dignity. I feel that I know her, and I want to help. Lifelessly watching me, her eyes seem to know me, too. Her eyes could be my mother's.

This face could be my mother's.

The heavy presence advances from my shoulders. It wraps around my throat and breathing is difficult. Am I breathing at all? My heart is not racing. I think it has stopped. Suddenly, eight long months of unfelt grief find me here on the sand in the cold July night.

Once more, a boat has sunk. Once more, passengers are brought for all the people to come and look for the faces of their kin. Once more, I am among these people. Only this time, a face has matched. Her eyes are darker than mine, though her skin is lighter. Her hair is a lovely mess, sticking out at angles.

It is not my mother's face, but it could be.

This lady with her pitiful, tattered headscarf and her lifeless, loving eyes; I see her. I really see her—do you know what I am saying? This woman's face, it could be my mother's face. After eight months of avoidance, I am now a lady whose heart breaks. My throat is the one which lets loose a wailing cry, and I myself feel very cold indeed.

Despite the pain which seeks to strangle me, my empty lungs empty further. I wail into a wicked night.

This coldness is a sadness I have never known before. But, it is a something like a knowing. It is that I have known the truth, but I have not accepted it. Now, it has violated me deeply and forced me to admit its power.

This knowing squeezes at my heart as to rupture it. This truth locks my knees tight as to force me to the ground. Then, it builds and it builds. Oh, have you ever known this feeling? I tell you, it is a hard thing to describe. My eyes release a torrent of tears, and my throat fails to hold back the wailing. Wailing, I feel myself again. The sinister presence cannot strangle me while my throat howls like this. The dying sound proves that I am alive: dying is not yet dead. By releasing, my heart might not explode from the pressure. If you have never heard a Swahili lady wail, well, my friend then you are very lucky indeed since you have not been as close to death as I am now.

It is for my mother that a prolonged, pained shriek escapes me. The word *mamangu*, once sacred to this child, becomes a twisted hurt. Deadly truth drums at my heart. Cold knowing expresses itself through chilling shouts which come from deep inside my own body somewhere. Some place of comfort is now broken in me.

Mamangu!

My mother!

My *mama!*

Other women near me see me and they see the lady with the face which could be my mother's. They do what Swahili ladies do, and they, too, begin to wail. Though, their wailing is softer than my own. My new reality—and loss of reality—is acknowledged in their own terrible shouts and cries.

They beg me *do not cry, do not cry*. We cry together and their hands reach out for me. *Do not cry, do not cry.*

My breathing is shallow between calls for my mother. *Do not cry, do not cry.*

The sorrow starts to drown me. *Do not cry.*

I have been a sturdy little boat. Now, I am a shipwreck. I am shattered, battered, soggy fragments. While crying keeps me alive, it lets that dark presence in closer. I am losing myself, and I simply accept it. My body is useless. My mind is broken. My spirit nears the same.

Then, different words are suddenly exclaimed.

"*We! Mtundu wee!*"

Wailing ladies are pushed aside. I am enveloped in two sturdy arms, and I am taken away from the tent. I am not taken far, but far enough that cold faces are no longer visible to me.

These enveloping arms belong to my neighbor, Bi. Mwinyi, who clasps my shoulders and turns me toward her. For a brief moment our eyes meet, which seems to be her intention, but mine are too full of shame and salty tears to remain. They dart downward to some dark spot in the sand.

Another call for my dead *mama* escapes my trembling lips.

"*Ah! We!* Stupid girl!" I am shaken by the strong arms of Bi. Mwinyi. Her hand then takes my chin and forces our eyes to meet again, firmly.

"Child, don't cry!" Her thumb is so firm in its grasp of my cheek. It hurts, and the physical pain distracts me. It reminds me of my existence. For a moment, the physical pain is stronger than spiritual pain. I am unsure which I prefer.

"Don't cry. Stop crying, oh, oh, oh."

Bi. Mwinyi takes me into her embrace and comforts me like the child that I am. The grip of the darkness is replaced by her grip on my shoulders. Her comfort holds me in place.

"Oh, oh, oh. Don't cry, ooh."

The low, drawing tone soothes my heart, and the wailing reduces to a quiet moaning.

"*Mama yangu*," my lips release a final time.

"—died, my child. Your mother has died, Tatu. Oh, oh, oh."

THURSDAY MORNING

"DA TATU! OH!"

This is my sister's voice, and it is very loud. But, I do not wish to heed her call.

"Tatu!"

Tatu. Yes, this is my name.

I have not told you before now because I have not thought that it was important to tell you. Tatu is not an unusual name, and it is not an interesting name.

In Swahili, it means 'three,' and it is a traditional name for girls who are born on Mondays. This is because Mondays, *Jumatatu*, are the third day of the week. You see, my name is very predictable, so I have not told you before now. I apologize.

I apologize to you, because I have wanted to keep you interested, and so I have neglected to tell you some things which visitors do not usually care to know. Instead, I have told you all the most interesting things. Of course, these are the things I keep in my trusted notepad.

When travelers come to Zanzibar, they want to hear the most interesting stories. They want to taste spices which they call 'exotic,' and they want to meet people who are very unlike themselves. Sometimes, they call those people 'exotic,' too. They want to meet sleepy, farting monkeys. They want to visit Jaws Corner and purchase porcelain cups of coffee from men who watch boisterous dramas. They prefer to avoid bad smells and piercing cries of wailing ladies.

Tourists on Unguja, they want to make single-file queues and walk through Darajani Market. There, they like to meet the handsome gentlemen who sell well-arranged packages of spices. They like to learn the ways to say 'cinnamon' and 'cloves' in Swahili. Visitors do not want to know about CUF or *Uamsho*, and they do not cross Haile Selassie Road. They do not stay in Ng'ambo. Tourists and travelers, they seldom reach Kiwimbi. Most of all, they would never stray onto a Kiwimbi replete with the bodies of passengers pulled from the deep, cold sea.

I have welcomed you as a traveler—a guest visiting Unguja. This is perhaps why I have made sure to tell you about all the most unusual and interesting people. Please do not think I have misled you, no. The ones whom I watch, they are also the most interesting people to me. I thought you may appreciate my observations.

Yes, I have done my best to show you a Zanzibar which might interest you. Granted, I have not told you about the spice farms or the tortoises on Prison Island, but those places are expensive. Forgive me. I have done my best to keep you from hearing painful sounds or seeing discomfiting sights.

But, now we are here. Accidents happen.

"*Da* Tatu, *wee!*"

"*Oh! Mama Nuru, haitiki!*" That is right, my sister, I am not responding.

I hear her feet walk away from the bedroom door—relief.

Perhaps I can try to tell you more things. After all, it is the usual things which make the unusual ones more special, isn't it? The maize porridge plays a part in the excitement for *biriyani*. Maybe the usual things make for more exciting unusual ones. I can share with you the ordinary events and the usual people. I can tell you about some things which tourists do not typically hear. Let us start with last night.

After she cradled me to her breast like a child, Bi. Mwinyi walked me away from Kiwimbi. I do not remember the journey at all, really, just pieces of the time—like photographs which cover some moments, but by their nature cannot preserve each and every feeling. Snapshots are saved in my memory like an album on a touch-phone. Between the pictures, there are gaps of forgotten feelings. Perhaps those gaps are panic, misery, screams and shouts; but they do not exist at all. I promise I am not withholding. Just snapshots of moments remain

For instance, I recall seeing faces of ladies around me in the tent as we departed. In this snapshot, all of their jaws are doing one of two things: either they are very tense and square as if they have bitten into a piece lime pickle or they are agape, mouths open in a turned-down crescent shape. Above despairing lips, their eyes are knowing eyes. I know them, too. I mean, I know that they feel for me. They recognize my sorrow, perhaps because they have known a sorrow like that once.

The next thing I can recall is seeing Mzee Ameir sitting on his stoop at the corner of our neighborhood. In that snapshot, it is more like a short video repeating on a loop. He does not greet us. Instead, he gravely nods his head. His forehead bows downward toward his chest. Then, it rises. It bows again. I think he, too, tries to demonstrate a knowing.

After that, I retain—and this is so silly—I retain so clearly an image of two chickens crossing the path in front of us. They approach the steps of Sheikh Kareem Mosque, but they do not dare enter. They are missing many feathers. I remember that. It is funny the things minds choose to remember, isn't it? I wonder if those mangled chickens can understand human sorrow. They do not look at me with knowing eyes or bowing heads.

I do not think they appreciate the intense pain around them, and maybe this is why I remember them. Because to them, last night is like any other night. For them, there is no tragedy. There is no unusual thing. Their lucky, chicken ignorance is proof that the world has not yet ended. I tell you, when the world is truly ending we will know it by the chickens and the small animals first. These creatures care for eating and for resting. Nothing else really matters. Just, they are surviving. When survival is so doomed that even the ignorant chickens panic—if they no longer care for eating and for resting—now, that day will be alarming, indeed.

After the blissful chickens, there are no more snapshots stored in my memory.

All throughout last night's journey, I know that Bi. Mwinyi was guiding me with a firm arm wrapped around my shoulder. However, I do not remember the walk and I do not recall entering our home. We might have even gone through the front door. I cannot say. Usually, of course, we girls enter through the courtyard and the kitchen—owh, now I am doing it again: focusing on unusual, 'exotic' things. Well, it is not for you but for me this time. Is this not different? It feels different.

Trying to remember does not feel happy, but it calms me somehow. My body is also sore, as if I had joined the exercising groups on the beach at Kiwimbi rather than cried under a tent. To be truthful with you, I feel like I am becoming ill. In the bottom of my belly, a pain grows. This pain draws my throat downward, and it dries out my mouth. Conversely, it moistens my eyes. It freezes me and threatens to eat me up from the tummy out.

Is this what being pregnant feels like? No, that cannot be. If I am pregnant, it is not with a happy, living thing. It is a dead thing. It is pain. I hold no desire to leave my bed. By the smell, Auntie has made *chila* and beans for breakfast, but I see no point in rising. The dead thing in my belly will not welcome bread or juice, I am sure. Besides, I do not want to feed it.

I say, I have been so good to tell you about unusual people. You know I have a talent for watching. My notes are well kept. I have been happy to share these stories with you. But, accidents happen. Ugly things happen. Sometimes, bad ugly things are more common than they are unusual. In this way, I have failed twofold. Not only have I shared with you a very nasty story, but it was not even an interestingly unusual one.

Here on Unguja, you see, we live on an island. If we want to go anywhere else, we go by plane or by boat. Likewise, if we want to go on a day-out or to visit cousins in *shamba* with their donkeys and mango trees, we go by shared car or bus. Plane, boat, car, bus—I tell you, it does not matter. Accidents happen, and they are not unusual. They are not interesting. Passengers sometimes do not survive. Well, passengers many times do not survive.

In fact, a ferry boat sank a few months ago in the same way one has done now. I have mentioned that to you already. I have not explained, though, that my mother was aboard that boat. I did not think it especially important to tell you. No one ever saw my mother after that accident. She was not among the cold bodies dutifully brought ashore. Thus, I cannot say with definite truth that Allah has taken her. Bi. Mwinyi and my auntie will tell you that He has.

Either way, we do not like to talk about the ones who have left us. I can tell you that my mother is gone, but I will never speak her name to you. And, I ask that you not speak her name to me. This is just how we Swahili people are, you must understand. Why discuss something so painful? Why begin something that can only end in crying? Reawakening tragedy only weakens a person, and allowing oneself to be weak like that—it is to invite bad spirits. Everyone knows this.

Those spirits, they will latch onto you in those times of weakness. They climb up onto your back, dig into your shoulders, and they make a home there. You see them in nightmares, and they haunt you. They show up in corners and windows, peeking out and always watching. I have even seen ladies who shriek and fall to the ground in the open street because their spirits torment them so horribly. I have told you how this sort of thing happens especially in these days just before Ramadhan.

However, you should not worry. Swahili spirits, they only bother the ones who believe in them. Spirits and djinns, they concern themselves only with the ones who concern themselves with them. That is what I have been taught. You need not give them any power by believing. Indeed, this is why you and I, we shall not discuss such painful things. Then, we will not have to worry about bad spirits and the ways they torment.

I trust that you understand, and we will not speak of it again.

In fact, the pain in my belly seems a lot like weakness now.

Taking a deep breath, I sit up. I forget about these feelings.

My feet find their way slowly to the floor. The tiles feel warm. Is it so late already? It must be, because July days are not quick to find their heat. By noon, they finally prepare a healthy serving of warmth for us, and my feet are telling me now that the floor has been warming for some time.

Though I am standing, I do not wish to join my sister and the others yet. However, my feet are taking me to the door. They are stubborn things, these feet, I tell you. My hand is turning the rusty knob—rusted like most anything metal that finds itself on Unguja for longer than a visit.

My sister squats on the other side of the door, sweeping dirt toward the kitchen with a hand broom, *fyu fyu fyuu*. That is the sound of its long bristles on our tiled floor. We normally use old *kanga*, wetting them lightly and pushing on hands and knees across the tiles. But, Bi. Mwinyi has given us this nice, sisal broom. It is nice because we do not have to crawl on knees and push with tired fingers. Instead, we just *fyu-fyu-fyu*, easy as whisking *kitumbua* batter. Bi. Mwinyi arrived with it one day a few months ago; a sisal broom in one hand, and our little brother in the other. She does seem to have a habit of returning us children when we stray, that one.

My sister flicks her wrist rhythmically. Some of the dirt lifts up into the air in front of me and I cough.

"Oh! Tatu *weye* you are sick."

I frown. No, I am not.

My sister scolds me, "Only sick people stay in bed like this. Stop your laziness!"

My frown extends to my eyes and I drop onto the mattress in the living room.

"No, no! Don't you see I am cleaning, get up!" she pushes at me like the stray animal I am—but if only. I might join the ignorant chickens and think just about eating and resting—well, mostly just resting today.

"Help me move this away now."

I oblige, and we hoist the mattress up onto one side. This thin, floppy piece of furniture is normally where I sleep along with my sister and little cousins if they stay the night. It is comfortable enough. In the cooler months, it is fine. But, I tell you, many January mornings I awake to a mattress damp with sweat. On those days, I find myself growing resentful of little cousins who stay the night. One body is hot enough on those nights when the moon is as hot as the sun, but four bodies on one mattress—oh, it is not easy.

During Ramadhan, one must relinquish any feelings like those of resentment. Auntie has always told me that this month is a time for cleansing. This sounds like cleaning, and so I imagine it is a similar thing. It is like cleaning but for minds and for spirits. At least the Holy Month this year falls during the cool season. Therefore, avoiding resentment of sweaty, little cousins should come naturally.

With two sets of arms and legs, moving the floppy mattress into Auntie's bedroom is a quick task. We finish sliding it through the doorway and deposit it, leaning against the wall like a tired, old lady. Poor mattress, it has seen so many nights of sleep and yet looks so worn. At least for those of us who do the sleeping, we regain some of our strength. It is clearly not so for the things on which we do the sleeping.

However, Auntie's bed is less threatened by multitudes of sweaty cousins. That mattress is one clean color all over and much less floppy. I surmise that I found myself in the bedroom last night thanks to Bi. Mwinyi installing me there after the march homeward.

Bi. Mwinyi is a good lady. She has always been so, but especially since the first ferry boat accident she has been around even more often. I have noticed this. Before, she would visit this time and that time, bringing bread but sometimes taking eggs. Since the accident, she has begun to sit and eat the bread with us girls. She takes eggs from Auntie less often. One time she actually brought us eggs. That was very unusual. Auntie kept a suspicious eye on her, but assuredly it seemed Bi. Mwinyi had no other motives but to share. She cares for us now.

Despite that care, it is still up to my sister and me to tidy the house each and every morning. Of course it is. Owh, my sister, her name is Dauda. Perhaps you are wanting to know it since I have told you mine. Perhaps you care about names now that you have had a taste of them.

Dauda is the second-born, but here at home she is the oldest. My brother lives in Dar es Salaam with his father. Therefore, my sister acts like she is the first-born and the most responsible. She scolds me, and tells me what it is that I ought to be doing. When we wake, she tells me to move the mattress away, and when we come home, she tells me to start preparing beans fast-fast.

Dauda is the second-born, which makes me—yes—the third. I am the third-born named *Three*. You may laugh. It is something others laugh about sometimes. In fact, it is nice that our brother lives in Dar, because many times people know only Dauda and so think I am the second-born after her. This way, my name is ordinary, but at least not something to laugh about. Until they ask me, and they learn that I am *Three*, the third child, born on the third day. You see how predictable I am. It is not interesting. My name and I, we are the maize porridge of girls.

My young brother also lives here with Auntie. If I am the ordinary, maize porridge of girls, then Fahad is the *biriyani* of boys. Fahadi is a small boy, but he is a large personality. He likes to dance, and sing songs he hears on the Indian and Venezuelan dramas. He finds kittens in the streets of Kiswandui and brings them home. These things frustrate Auntie, but she has long since stopped trying to change Fahadi's ways. He is a very stubborn boy, and the things he does can be unusual.

The way Fahad looks is unusual, too. Many people call him *mchina* because of this, but he is not really Chinese. Fahad's father came from Malaysia to Zanzibar when I was a young girl. Our mother started to spend time with him. I do not know exactly when. But, he came to our house a few times. Then, one day he left. He did not come to our house again, and we have not seen him since then. To be truthful with you, I do not mind. Fahadi's father was not kind to me, and I was not kind to him. I did not like how our mother became when he was around.

When our mother would spend time with Fahadi's father, she would speak to me less. I think this is because Fahad's father would not speak to me at all. I suppose that man was like the Sun or the Earth. He was having a type of gravity like great, enormous things do, and my mother moon fell into his gravity. She would spin around him so: a shooting star trapped in orbit of an ugly planet, destined to revolve around him until she herself burned away into cold, dull rock.

Our mother spun around that ugly man into places she would not go before he entered our family's orbit—or we entered his. I remember Auntie sucking her teeth in some telling way while our mother spun out the door, across the street, and into a CCM bar. Fahad's father liked to go to bars.

I remember these things. Sometimes, I remember these things when I look at Fahadi. When this happens, I feel badly. This is how I feel because it is not Fahadi's fault. In fact, he has never met his father at all. None of that ugly man with all of his gravity was part of raising him from birth, no. He might have had gravity powerful enough to trap our mother, but he does not exist in Fahadi's universe—not even a distant satellite. And, this way is better. Our mother, Auntie, Dauda, and me, we were the parts that mattered. Bi. Mwinyi and others, too, of course were there.

This is how Swahili families help each other. We do not discriminate with divisive terms like 'stranger' or 'distant cousin'. We help each other because we are together. I do not miss Fahadi's father because he did not seem to understand this about us. He is a distant planet now.

Now, I look at Fahadi as he plays with one of his clandestine kittens. This one is very little. I tell you, if this cat found itself in a fight with a mouse I think the mouse would be the winner! It is dirty, too.

"*We!* Wash this one or it will make us all sick," Dauda scolds him.

Fahadi pays her no attention and walks away from us into Auntie's bedroom. He is truly a strange boy, that one.

"*Mtundu*," Dauda gives voice to my thinking. Selfishly, I admit it is nice to hear '*mtundu*' said and find myself not to be the target.

Dauda says *mtundu* very often. Owh, this word, it means 'stupid' or 'silly.' It means 'stupid' when Dauda says it to Fahadi. It means 'silly' when Bi. Mwinyi says it to me. I cannot explain how to tell the difference, but I assure you that there is a difference. Just, sometimes it is more harsh than others.

At this moment, Auntie walks in through the back door. That is the door which opens to the courtyard where we cook on stoves and hang washing to dry. Do not worry, though, smoke from cooking rarely leaves a stench on our clothes. We are close enough to the sea to be blessed with cool breezes. Salty air gently rushes in, scoops up the smoke from frying fishes, and takes it somewhere away from our clotheslines.

Sometimes, neighbors burn rubbish down on the edge of the football field. Auntie's house is sort of on a cliff, you see, and a field we call Castro lies down at the bottom of the impossibly steep climb. One side of that natural wall is covered with rubbish. Plastics, fabrics, frayed ropes; they all find their final resting place there. Every now and then, someone deems the pile too wearisome and they light a fire to it. This is fine. There are few solutions to getting rid of things on an island. Fire is a quick one.

Though, it is not so fine for us who live here atop the hillside. Ashes rise up from the rubbish blaze and land in our courtyard. It is too unpleasant. But, there are few solutions on an island. We cannot neglect our washing. Others cannot neglect the rubbish heap. What else is there to do? We are together, and we cannot help that our burning conflicts with our washing.

I doubt it is washing that Auntie comes in from now. She leaves that chore to me and Dauda. Auntie, she is content to cook and beat lessons into our bottoms. Those are her preferred chores. To be truthful with you, I suspect that Auntie would sooner hire a girl to do the washing before doing it herself at all. She plays that the task is simply beneath her, but me, I think she is simply not wanting to do it. Perhaps she is even bad at handwashing! I have never seen her do it, so I cannot say.

"There are two basins full of washing! Just sitting in their filth!"

"Tatu *wee*!"

Enh, you see? Today is not different than any day. Accidents may happen and girls may wail, but Auntie stays the same.

"*Bee*," I acknowledge her from down the hallway.

"You are going to do the washing. Isn't it?"

"*Naam*, mama," I comply.

She nods a stern face. My compliance spares me further shouting, but not so for a Fahadi who reemerges from Auntie's own bedroom. He has the kitten cupped in his two hands. Its hair is especially tousled from his overeager handling. The smallest squeak escapes it before Auntie begins a shouting, and Fahad dashes past her for the courtyard door.

"You will leave that one outside! You will come back here right now!"

Another feline squeak, this time prolonged and fearful, can be heard through the window.

"*Mtundu*," adds Dauda.

Suddenly, the kitten creeps into the corner of my vision. I glance downward, but it is not there. In fact, it cannot have been Fahadi's kitten. I have just told you how he has taken it out to the courtyard in his hands, cupped tightly. Light plays tricks on sleepy eyes. Anyway, the thing was not kitten-shaped at all. Have you seen vines which creep around tree trunks or up the sides of buildings? The thing I have seen is like that—like shadows of vines, creeping until I look and then there is nothing to be seen.

That is too strange. I rub the sleep, and the creeping shadows, from my eyes. I blink three heavy, deliberate blinks. I can forget funny tricks of light, but I cannot forget the feeling. While I blink away shadows, a lurking discomfort remains with me.

In the base of my neck, a tenseness pinches at me. Just, I feel uneasy. It is difficult to describe: like a presence rests just behind me, and I consider casting sideways glances to check over my shoulders. At the same time, I do not want to know. Most of all, I know that no presence is truly there. Tricks of light and anxious pinches are not real company. They are just what they are, and to think otherwise is foolishness. It is weakness. Forgive me.

My arms wrap around my middle and squeeze me gently. I am just where I am and I forget about funny shadows. Inhaling, I look to see where it is that Dauda has gone.

Auntie stands in the courtyard doorway, waving an authoritative finger at Fahadi. Dauda has gone into the kitchen. My feet take me to her. Kneeling on the tiles, she is looking for something on the lowest shelf of the refrigerator. My head rests on my shoulder to get a better view. The electricity goes out.

"*Huuooo!*"

"Ah!" Auntie turns away from her hopeless battle with Fahadi in the courtyard and faces us inside.

"What is this? It is not even evening. *Inshaallah* we are not going without it for a week this time, *jamani…*"

With the refrigerator light extinguished, Dauda lets loose a losing sigh. I try to read her face.

"What are you looking for?"

For my curiosity, I receive a sneer.

"You have been told to do the washing. I'll find the mango pickle for lunch. The electricity will come back."

"Mmh."

You see, Dauda is more alike Auntie than I. She does what a girl is supposed to do at the time she should be doing it. She believes in systems and plays by rules. Dauda, she has been fasting like a proper Muslim lady for five years now. When electricity goes out unexpectedly, she trusts that it is part of Allah's plan, and she knows work must go on as usual despite the increased darkness. Every day, she wakes early, moves the mattress away, cleans the floors, prepares rice and beans, and disciplines Fahadi when Auntie abandons trying to find him.

To be truthful, sometimes I am only frustrated because I cannot begin to do all the things she does. She is very efficient—like Auntie, but a version of Auntie who also does the washing. When my using too much Omo ruins a skirt or when my clumsy hands noisily knock over a bowl I am envious of Dauda's skillful focus. I want to tell you that she is this way since she is older and has had more years of practice. I want to tell you that, but I am unsure if it is the truth.

On the other hand, Dauda has not been to school for many years. She is well educated in maintaining a home and caring for clumsy siblings, but her English does not compare to mine or Asha's. Her maths are only good when she is in the market. I tell you, she counts eggplants and multiplies them by their price with impressive quickness. But, she does not know what a fraction is, nor a decimal.

The thing about Dauda, though, is that she is good at the things she is good at while she has no time for the others. Me, I am good at carefully looking at others and reading them. I read people's stories like they are open books. Dauda certainly cannot do that. But, she can discipline naughty children—they obey her. She can fix lamps and stoves which seem beyond repair to me. My sister, she is good at these things, but must I be? I believe it is expected of me, but I cannot find joy in it.

Me, I find joy in looking at the ones who do unusual things. I watch them, and I determine why it is that they do the things they do and are the ways they are. I learn truths about people. Is there no value in that skill? Looking at the sea; I enjoy that, too. From the safety of the solid shore, I like the way the waves repeat themselves. With minimal differences, they continually crash over coral. Others fear the deep, dark waters, but I can see that they are predictable. They follow patterns. In this way, waves and people are the same. Despite the loud noises they make, they are quite simple.

I do not feel simple, myself. As for Dauda, I think she is simple. She is like a regularly sized wave that follows all the similarly sized waves before her. Thanks to Auntie-sized waves, she knows the rigid path forward—what comes next and how to prepare. From mother-sized waves, she has learned how to guide the young waves who follow her—myself, Fahadi. What of myself and Fahadi, though? If we are there in the sea with Dauda we are not regular, predictable waves.

Fahadi is like a flying fish who flits below and above the waves. They cannot restrain him. Indeed, he is limited only by his reckless imagination. And me, what am I? I am resistant to that pull which guides Dauda, but I am not constantly lost like Fahadi. Our mother, I might ask her what she thinks. I might ask her to tell me who or where I am.

However, this is not possible. I cannot ask her. Foolishly, I am in these thoughts again. My belly sinks into a hollow feeling. My heart is squeezed tightly, softly beating. I have no appetite, but my insides are painfully empty. My arms wrap around my middle once again, and I close my eyes.

"*Weye*, have you not been told multiple times now?"

My eyes open. In her right hand, Dauda holds a jar packed with the softest slivers of green mango. With her left hand, she throws fingers toward the courtyard.

"Go now, *basi*, do it!"

My feet reluctantly take me to the doorway despite the suspicious pinching at my neck. My jaw aches a little, too. Owh, the teeth farthest back in my mouth have been grinding—for how long? Well, it has been long enough to ache.

Bending to avoid a line of damp *kanga*, I enter the courtyard. Two basins full of clothes are resting patiently here, as Auntie has described. I admit, there is nothing else to do. At least, I can do some washing. Washing clothes is a daily thing. It is not special. If I give this ordinary span to Auntie, she should not think I give her the whole measure. Still, it would be nice to have the *kanga* with that caption. I could have worn it now while I wash. I could have asserted my firm independence.

Instead, here we are. Here, heaving a yellow water can from one end of the narrow courtyard to the other. I do not pour it so much as knock it. Using my legs' momentum, I toss the can onto the first basin. *Ga guu ga gung'* its contents slosh back and forth until they submit to gravity. The water inside spits unevenly onto our clothes. It is the pale color of bottled things that men drink at the CCM bars, this water. This is its color since it does not come from the delivery trucks. No, it comes from the tap closer to the airport road beside Bwana Usi's house.

Of course, Dauda must have been to the water tap while I have been sleeping. I bet you that she makes mention of this later. She is going to use it against me. Dauda calls me the harsh form of *mtundu* and she tells me to stop my laziness, but I am not lazy! You must not believe her words. Dauda, she is just not normal. Rather, perhaps she is just too normal. Fahad and I make our renegade path through patterned waves. Dauda is the wave. You see, it is not my fault. I cannot be a thing which I am simply not.

The first basin fills nicely, so I contemplate the second one. Why has it been filled up with clothes, too? Auntie, she really leaves this task to me. Oh, she does not even think sense! We do not have any more than these two basins. I need them both for the washing. Casting a cautious eye toward the doorway, I see that I am alone here, so I overturn the second basin and dump its clothes onto the cement. This is fine—the ground is not dirty here thanks to Dauda's ceaseless sweeping—but, I must work quick to keep my covers from blowing.

The first basin is not quite full up with clothes, so I pick a few things from my newly made pile and add them in. Next, my hands push and they push. They get everything nicely wet. Then, it is time for soap. My fingers gather a pinch of the powder and shake it over the basin. Repeating themselves, my hands push and push. This part is my least favorite. Owh, do not misunderstand me, I have no favorite part.

I mean to say, I dislike the way soap makes my skin feel. At first, it makes the clothes feel like smooth, slippery fish in the water. Unfortunately, we do not finish there. My hands must take up one piece of clothes at a time. The right hand takes hold of one end of a *shungi*. Its counterpart takes hold of the other, and they rub together. Gripping fabric tightly, fingers thrust it against the heel of the opposing hand.

Eventually, this repetitive cycle of washing leaves my hands raw. Clothes are purified, but skin is damaged. From all of yesterday's writing, my fingers already mildly ache. My hands accept their fate. Mild aches increase and are joined by red hatch marks. Along with her black gloves, this is how Auntie maintains her skin's softness. Other ladies are fooled into thinking that she knows secrets of the best moisturizing creams. Me, I know that she only knows secrets of forced labor.

After some dozen pushes of the *shungi's* black fabric against itself upon my wrist my hands turn to wringing. They fold the soggy cloth and spin it hard– but, not too hard as to tear or wrinkle it. They wring it just firmly enough to expel all the excess water. Tap water oozes out. Its pale brownish color is made at least a little more pleasant by the white Omo powder.

Three *shungi* are tossed into the second basin, filled with clean water. To that, my hands add Fahad's uniform, his underpants, and his trousers. They deposit Auntie's favorite headscarf and Dauda's black housedress. The *kanga* come last, since they are prone to bleeding color. It is better to scrub and wring them over a basin whereby other nice clothes cannot be accidentally dyed funny shades of pink or yellow. This, I have learned from past errors. I have found that a beaten bottom is an especially effective way to remember past errors.

After all the clothes are securely in the basin of pure, plain water my hands do some more pushing. They must sit, the excess Omo seeping out into the water. For now, I leave them to it. There is only so much pushing hands can do. Sometimes, things must sit and take their time for a bit. More action does not always mean more results.

Like the clothes, now I sit. I wait. If only the excess soap could seep out from my hands' poor skin as it does from the damp fabrics. Well, I could sit with my hands immersed in some other clean water. That seems absurd, though. I am a girl, not a pair of trousers. I do not think it works the same way.

Therefore, I find space below the bedroom window and I sit. If Auntie has not gone out into the neighborhood or to the market, then she is likely there on the other side of this window. With my bottom against the wall, I am hidden from sight. My arms gently pull my knees to my chest, and I rest my chin nestled between them.

Doing this washing has been good. My aches are less noticeable, and my shoulders are less strained by funny, worrying feelings. Yes, my fingers throb and my palms are a little worn, but maybe it is these pains which dull the others by comparison. Even my stomach is lighter. In fact, it is empty.

Lifting up from bent knees, my chin turns curiously toward the stove. My eyes can see that flames are licking angrily at a large, round pot. This one is probably full of rice. My ears do not detect rolling, bubbling sounds of boiling water, so I suspect that the rice is almost ready.

Just now, a light illuminates the bedroom window above me. The electricity has returned. That was not so long. A collective '*huoooo!*' can be heard from all the children in the neighborhood. I allow myself a small smile. It is good, because water pumps can lift water up into tanks and electric stoves can light. These resources are particularly precious today, I am sure, since so many aunties and mamas prepare their homes for Ramadhan. In our home, we do not have an electric stove to make cooking an easier task, but we do have a water pump. With a turn of a switch, it whirs and hums. It sends dozens of liters up a pipe, into our great, black tank which lives atop our courtyard wall.

Sometimes, I have had to climb up and mend a little valve where the pipe meets the tank. I tell you, it is a scary thing only because standing there, a girl can see straight down the hillside, which as I have told you, is much more a cliff than a hill. The sight of that height makes my feet choose their moves very, very carefully. It reminds me that I am small and fragile. However, I am not so scared. Truthfully speaking, I find speaking to strangers more daunting than climbing steep walls next to cliffs.

Fortunately, speaking to strangers is seldom necessary. Granted, responding to greetings is a given. When someone greets me as I walk on my way, I must reply accordingly. To ignore the words of an elder would be especially shameful. Still, this is different than really having to speak to a person. I do not speak to people very much when I can just watch them and learn all the same things that might be gleaned from an uncomfortable conversation.

Now, I contemplate my notepad again. After last night's events, has it found its way back into the oldest sock in Dauda's drawer? I have not thought to check until now. More likely, it remains in my blouse's breast pocket in a heap by the bed. That is where I put it last, and Bi. Mwinyi does not know that it belongs stuffed in the dresser drawer in that particular sock. In fact, unless Dauda has begun paying more attention, no one but me knows that spot, either. Thus, it must be wrapped up in the blouse.

Knowing this should be a relief. My carefully collected stories are secure where I have left them. My chest does not sigh in relief, and my heart does not beat with anticipation. Instead, my belly is empty. When I think of carefully watching unusual people, it normally provokes a certain feeling in my belly, just below my chest. This feeling of anticipation is like a gentle, little fire. It is like a fire which does not burn or harm. Instead, it only warms. It lights me up and guides me toward action.

Today, instead of that warming spark my belly feels nothing at all. The warmth has been stolen away. The more I think about the hollowness, the more it becomes a painful thing. The more the pain eats at me, the more isolated I am where I sit. My chin digs into my knees and my arms squeeze my legs into my chest. There is no remedy. Loss is better unspoken, lest spirits weaken. Weak spirits are prey to stronger, unkind ones—the ones with nightmares for eyes and long, sharp fingers. We do not discuss loss here for this reason. We must stay strong. We must not give up our energy to dark feelings.

All this effort to be strong leaves me feeling weakened. There has to be a better way. Washing has done a good job of distracting me. Is that it? Distraction is the solution. I must distract myself until I can no longer remember anything that leaves me empty or susceptible to dark feelings. I could become like

Dauda, dedicating myself to washing, tidying, and cooking. This way, all of my spare moments would be consumed by distraction. I could become like Fahadi, never standing still. The next curiosity and adventure would guide me away from any thoughts of difficult accidents in the past. I could live only in the present moment.

Truthfully, I do not think either path is ideal. But, I cannot tell you a better solution. For now, all I can tell you is that my belly's hollow pains are a little less noticeable when my chin digs into my thighs. When my arms squeeze my legs tighter, I feel that I am still a solid, human body, at least. Because I feel physical pain, I know that I am still here. Though my existence is painful, I know that it is one.

All this effort to exist in this place leaves me feeling worn. I have kept my mind here where it belongs in my body, but at what cost to my spirit? I am woefully tired. I cannot begin to think of going out and watching unusual people. Leaving home at all seems like a burdensome feat. For today, I will take the Dauda path of distraction. Emerging from the red-colored dent it has pressed into my skin my chin lifts again.

My eyes consider the pot of rice. My ears are picking up on a new sound emanating from inside, *se see seeh*. This is not the sound of boiling, no. It is the shrill hissing of rice which burns.

Committing to distraction, I leap up and busy myself with the work. A tattered, fragment of *kanga* lies trapped under the wash basin. One firm tug liberates it. Then, I wrap it around the lid's handle. This handle, it is more of a nub, really. For as long as I have known it, I have known it to be a half-handle. It does the same job, nonetheless.

Regardless, it gets too hot for me. I need a barrier of cloth between skin and tin. I have seen Bi. Mwinyi lift this same lid by its nubby handle without any cloth at all. That one, her skin wears decades of blistered, toughened armor. Even Dauda cannot reach into flames and calmly clasp hot metal like Bi. Mwinyi can. With age and womanhood come peculiar strengths, I suppose. Me, I have many, many days of busying myself with distraction before my hands can rival Bi. Mwinyi's. For today, I opt for a little bit of protection.

Relieving the pot of its stifling lid looses a cloud of steam. I give the lid one sturdy shake, and the hot moisture disperses. A bounty of basmati hisses within. There is no moisture left in there, only rice. Right in the middle, the top layer has turned golden and crispy. That part is my favorite. I like the way it breaks in my teeth. Deep at the bottom of the pot where rice sits too long and approaches a texture like porridge, that is Fahadi's favorite. He eats it late at night instead of sleeping when Auntie tells him to do. When he can find milk, he mixes the rice with that, too. Then he sleeps and farts like a little Colobus monkey.

Owh, but, I have not thought this thoroughly through. Where to set the lid for this next step? These things are Dauda's specialty. My *kanga*-covered hand searches for a clean place. I cannot move the pot from the three rocks on which it perches while my right hand holds this thing. It is larger than the full width of my shoulders, and the pot is the same plus a day and a half of basmati's weight. One day, I will be as wide as Bi. Mwinyi and maybe then I can move a pot with one hand and hold a lid with the other, both without *kanga*—tough skin only, oh!

However, that version of me is not today's me. My hand abandons any creative solution, and replaces the lid where it has found it. Then, I bend at the knees to heave the pot up with both hands.

My left hand scalds and I shriek, falling onto my bottom.

"Oh!" Dauda's voice calls from inside. Do not confuse this with concern. It is a noise responding to a stimulus. In fact, I do not respond and she does not venture out to the courtyard. You see? This is how we are sometimes. Not every sound has meaning.

Anyway, back to business, I tighten the *kanga* around my right hand. Pulling another *kanga* from the wash basin, I wrap that around the other. My knees bend again, and my hands grip the sides of the pot.

This time, I have got it. Knees straighten. I deliver the pot closer to the doorway, but my left hand starts to feel hot. It feels very, very hot—somehow, even hotter than before! A shriek escapes me again, and this time it is the rice pot who falls to the ground. It clangs loudly, a booming sound, and the lid soars into a wall. That, too, crashes like an unwelcome, brass orchestra.

My right hands flings its protective cloth away, and tears at the wet one on my left. It is as hot as a fire now. Touching it only leads to twice as many hands in pain, so I whirl my entire arm in the air until the damp, smoldering *kanga* unravels and smacks against the wall, much like the lid. Though, its sound is less of an orchestra and more of a dead fish.

Again Dauda calls out, "Oh!" This time, she is in the doorway.

"*Mtundu weye! Si huwezi kuangalia chochote peke 'ako!*"

She slaps my hand—the unburnt one, at least. She spies the lid, the wet *kanga*, and the uncovered pot of rice. Shrugging hopelessly, she sucks her teeth at my mess. I find myself cowered against the high wall, feeling smaller and emptier.

"You have to do just the washing. Why are you even touching the rice?"

She regards me with crazed eyes. She has learned this look from Auntie.

"You just mess it up."

She throws the lid back onto the pot, and returns to the kitchen.

I slide myself over to the wash basin and insert my left hand. It is not too badly burnt, but the water is soothing.

Perhaps keeping busy is not meant for me. Me, I am not an obedient wave like Dauda. I cannot follow the predictable, patterned trails set for me. You see me: I have tried, and look what happens! Who am I meant to be in this sea? I begin to think I am the driftwood.

Do you know it, the one like dry bones which entangles itself in slimy plant matter and debris? It is only good for helplessly floating. If I am not a steady, little wave nor a reckless, flying fish, then perhaps I am that one. Floating along, I pick up the remains of others' stories. They attach to me by accident. One day eventually, I will make landfall and then I will dry out in the hot sun. Things happen to me. They do not happen by me.

Again, I wonder. I think of our mother, and I wonder what she might say to me. Would she call me driftwood? Would she tell me to stand up and be a woman? I can never know. I cannot ask her.

Again, my surroundings fall away and I live in a dark space in my own mind. Shoulders tense and a hole burns where my belly should be. An island is what I am. An island on an island who is very much alone. Someone—something—else's hands grip my shoulders at the base of my neck. It intends to stay there. Sinisterly, it dares me to tell anyone about my agony—to tell them and have it swallow me up, whole. My own hands reach around my legs and pull them against chest. I close my eyes. Let it end, if it must be like this. Eyes moisten. Teeth grind.

FRIDAY MORNING

"DA TATU! TATU, OH! DA Taaatuu wee!"

Startled, I awaken as a solid thing bluntly presses into my ribs. Opening with great difficulty, my eyes construe the solid thing to be Dauda's foot.

"You have overslept again. You are really sick!"

I murmur a disagreement.

"No? Get up, then."

I roll away from her onto the floor, and she heaves the mattress up onto its side, by herself. Dauda is strong when she wants to be—or when she is emotional. She must be angry with me now.

My knuckles rub sleep from my eyes, which blink deeply. To be truthful with you, I barely recollect time's passage from yesterday to now. It has been a blur of stomach pain and tenseness. The wicked thing perched on my back—invisible to anyone else, apparently—has really sunk in its claws.

"You are not going to help me at all?"

Rising to my feet, I place hands on my side of the upright mattress. Elbows crookedly stabilize the floppy thing. It makes its way into the hall and then into Auntie's bedroom. Usually, we do a graceful shimmy to fit the length through the narrow doorway. This time, Dauda is in a rush. She forcefully bends the mattress around the doorframe. We deposit it in its regular spot, leaning against the wall.

I rest my bottom atop Auntie's bed, much firmer than our flimsy, mobile mattress. Dauda looks down at me with surprise. Unsure what it is she is wanting, I look at her plainly. Her eyes widen with expectation.

"It is like you are possessed, girl!"

"Ah!" I protest.

"These days, you are only lazy. Come on."

She opens a drawer in Auntie's dresser, and pulls out something that sounds unmistakably like crinkling, paper money. She thrusts a handful of small bills into my right hand.

"Auntie is sending you to the market," she explains, "we need hibiscus and spices."

Why so early? Anyway, the courtyard is already busy with smells of cooking. Even from this innermost bedroom, my nose detects cardamom and cumin.

"But the pilau is already cooking. Why does she want spices now?"

"For next week, *mtundu*. Or do you want to go during Ramadhan when every *bibi* is there in a grumpy state—shopping on empty bellies? Owh, get the hibiscus flowers from the Arab—not from Bi. Neema this time. Have you heard me?"

Yes.

"*Wee*, have you heard me, oh?"

"Yes."

She is so pushy.

Dauda directs her feet toward the courtyard, and I contemplate the shillings in my hand. They are two thousand, five hundred. All are 500-shilling bills. Abeid Amani Karume's face is looking up at me from the green paper. He has a nice face, I have always thought this. He has round cheeks like me and kind eyes like Fahadi. It is too bad that he holds his space on the smallest bill.

Surely, Zanzibar's first president deserves a higher worth. The green is good, though. Green is the color of paradise. But, why not put Bw. Karume on the 5,000-shilling bill, and the green go with him? The 5,000 has a purple rhinoceros. Neither this color nor this animal are common, anyway. Then, the purple rhinoceros will be on the 500 and the green Karume will be the second largest. But, no, this is the way our union works, you see.

I cannot imagine President Karume looking up at me from a large bill. Some mainlanders would not appreciate an islander holding so much value. We are a union, but they are more numerous. It has been that way since Auntie's aunties were little children. In fact, Bi. Mwinyi has told me that President Karume himself signed the deal to make it so. Since then, we have been a union of mainland and island. Karume became the union's vice president after that.

To me, it is not clear how the *wauamsho* feel about President Karume. I know that Bwana Usi has mentioned their disgust with the government, but I think that applies to today's government. I know that they want the islands to wake up and become independent. To me, that seems like Bwana Karume's old deal is very much against what they want.

For now, Karume stays on the little 500 bill, the smallest of them all. It is alright, though, it means his friendly face is the one I see most often. Though, even five of him amounts to only 2,500 and this will be a challenge at the market. For spices, I have to visit Darajani, and with this amount I have to bargain.

All of this seems like such a heavy burden. Staying home, I cannot be surprised. No boats can sink indoors. If I stay home, I will not see any lifeless bodies—as long as I do not turn on the TV. It is safest here. Really, during Ramadhan I have no reason to be anywhere else. Just, I could stay the whole month. There is no school. No one will need me to be outside more than I need me to be safe in here. Is it crazy thinking?

"You have not left yet!" Dauda calls mockingly from the courtyard.

If I must go out, then I do it on my terms. We already know that I am not meant to be an obedient wave. If I must go out into the sea this morning, then let me be like Fahad. He is never bothered. Like a flying fish, he flits below and above the waves. He is unrestrained and untethered. I have seen how he plays. Every moment is all the same to him. He lives in the present, and when a situation is unpleasant—well, he just leaves. Where is Fahadi now, anyway? Typically, he is unaccounted for.

Anyway, my feet are first to give in to our inevitable journey. They stand me upright, and I cooperate with my knees who lower me to Dauda's drawer in the dresser. Today, I am not a wave at all but a fish who rides whichever waves she likes. I am above it, and part of it when I choose to be.

Inspired, I withdraw the oldest sock, but it is empty of its treasure. Owh, my notepad is still wherever Wednesday's blouse has been. I scurry around the bed. At this moment, Dauda passes the doorway and rolls her eyes at my mischief. That is just how she is.

Here, it seems my blouse, black but noticeably a little dirty, has stayed. If it had been anywhere else during this time, Dauda would have collected it and added it to the washing. Because it is here by chance beside Auntie's bed, I think she has left it out of respect. She cannot possibly think such a size belongs to Auntie. Regardless, I am glad it is here and my notepad is not soggy in a basin, but safe and dry.

Unfolding the fabric, I feel the little book inside its pocket. I take it out and a smile returns to me for what seems like the first time in a while, isn't it? Yes, let me be like the unstoppable flying fish and let me go do what it is that I do best. I exist uniquely—an unusual girl. I exist, but I am separate, bouncing around and gleaning what is to be seen from my watching.

I replace the notepad and wrap a scarf over my head. This one is a yellow like banana-flavored candies. In Auntie's tall, narrow mirror I can see that a tuft of naughty hair is peeking out above my brow. A finger stuffs it back into proper hiding.

My finger runs along the edge of my hood, ensuring it is all folded proper. As it does so, I catch a glimpse of something in the mirror. My stomach lurches sideways. It feels as if my heart has flipped its top toward bottom and bottom on top.

Here, in the corner of the mirror I have seen something. Something—a someone—a thing, it has been just here, but now it is gone. I tell you, it has had a face. Rather, it has eyes: big, bulbous eyes without any expression in the middle of a pointed space—pointed at the top and at the bottom. This is not a human face.

No.

My mind plays tricks on me. All the same, I am frightened. I have seen it. It was here. It is here. And, it has seen me. Those eyes looked right at me—like a thing that knows me—a thing from a different place—not this world.

No, no, oh no—I have always been told—and I have told you, too. The things that are not there—but are there—they do not bother the ones who do not think of them. Me, I am not believing in things like that. Me, I am not believing in bad spirits—in *majini*—in *mashetani*. I am not believing in them, and so they cannot bother me. This is how it goes.

I want to close my eyes and make it all dark for a moment. I want to close my eyes; but truthfully, I am anxious about what is going to be there when I open them again.

A tune rises up from my chest, and I hum.

Mm-enh-mh-mm, my feet reluctantly escort me to the hallway. *Enh-mh-mm-mh,* here there are only things I can see, and I am not believing in spirits. *Enh-mhh,* I am believing in these walls and these tiles and two feet below me. These are the things I can feel and see. These things are the ones I think about—just what is here in front of me.

"You are not a good singer."

Dauda walks back the other way, toward the courtyard.

"You have a job to do, isn't it?"

Yes, pushy sister, it is. It is.

Yesterday has reminded me of what I am not. I am not Dauda. She might find purpose in rigid routine. Me, I cannot manage it. That lifestyle is for less independent people. As we know, I am independent.

I am not driftwood. I cannot be a thing that floats and has all the things happen to it. That one, it is weak. It has a bad smell, too.

Today, I try a new strategy. Today, I am like a flying fish. Unlike Dauda and the stiff, little waves, I can break through the dark waters. Like a flying fish—like Fahad—I am free because I choose to be. I am above all this usual, dull darkness.

My eyes locate a pencil near the TV stand. It is a nicely sharpened one, too. It is not an ink pen, but it achieves what I need. I must cross the path of a small mirror to reach it—owh, and the darkened television screen, itself. It seems so vast now. It is worse than a mirror, even—so black. I have not noticed this about it before. From my belly rises another humming.

Mm-enh-mm-mm, my eyes squint so that I do not have to catch any glimpses of mirror or TV screen. My hand swiftly snatches the pencil, and my feet turn quickly away from the spot. We make for the front door.

"*Haya*! I am coming. Later!"

Dauda shouts a nonverbal response to the stimulus, acknowledging my noise. My right hand turns the doorknob, and my left undoes the lock. My heart is lifted a little upon realizing that my left hand feels alright after yesterday's little accident. No burns seem to have set in. Shutting the door behind me, followed by the metal gate, I depart.

A second realization comes to me as I know that for a heart to rise it must first have fallen. The feeling of my heart lifting has meant that it was feeling unusually low just before. But, I brush gloomy thoughts aside. Today, I am like a carefree fish who flies above dark waters. Those gloomy waters cannot pull me down to their level—not today, *jamani*.

Outside the courtyard door, Fahad is sitting in the dirt. Fahadi is about exactly half Dauda's age, and he is just larger than half my size. When he balls his fingers up into a fist, I can fit his whole hand into mine. I think he has a small stature from his father. Certainly, his silky hair comes from him, and a natural penchant to curl from our mother. As for his behaviors, I do not know where he gets this—perhaps from our mother. But, the way he dances on the edge of his toes is not a thing he has learned from her. The way he sings *bongo flava* songs is especially showy. He is a unique boy, this one.

At present, his little fingers weave through green leaves he has collected. I do not understand what it is that he is doing, but this is nothing new. Rather, I feel that two carefree beings such as us, we should unite.

"I am going to the market. Will you come?"

He looks up from his nonsense for a moment, but shakes his head.

Well, I should not be surprised. Anyway, carefree fish are free of cares. One does not require a companion. That is quite against the point, isn't it?

With this mindset, I turn on my heels and make my way over the mound which lies between Auntie's house and Sheikh Kareem. My feet are treading confidently for I have fit them into closed shoes today. Ramadhan is coming and the house has been particularly clean lately. I know that I ought to keep it that way. Bare toes in sandals seek out mud and dust like Fahadi seeks out stray creatures. They are drawn to each other.

You see, it is better to cover them up and reduce my chances for trouble later. A girl can still be free while her toes are not, I assure you. A girl can be independently minded beneath extra fabric.

In fact, the extra coverage on my toes makes for quick work of traversing the mound. Stable feet descend its other side, and I pass the grand mosque to my left side. Its white steps, though exposed to the dust and the sun, are just as clean as the living room floor Dauda has so expertly scrubbed. Five pillars line the open entrance to the mosque. A few older men are kneeling inside. They are early for *adhuhuri* prayer.

Where Kikwajuni ends, the football fields begin. Next to the gym, I spy the young men who eagerly greeted the boys who make plans. Those young men make me nervous. But today, I do not mind them. They may do what they please because I am doing what I please. Today, I am above the choppy seas. No one can pull me down.

Next, I reach Jamhuri Gardens. They are mostly empty at this time. Swings hang still in the calm air. A crow lands on the rusty leopard statue, and harshly caws. It faces directly toward me and makes its awful sound one more time before lifting and finding a new perch on a flimsy, blue slide. Since it is nearly noon, I expect that most people are on their way to mosque for Friday prayer. You see what a natural rebel I am? Me, I swim against the current. I have a job to do.

My feet follow the aging fence which encloses the gardens. Tangled brush pokes out from above and between. At the end of this fence, the gardens open up to the widest road; the one that connects Michenzani to Stonetown. On this one, it is wide enough for motorbike riders to race. I have heard them doing this at the latest hours of the night. Crossing this road is stressful. However, today I am unencumbered. I find a confident lady by whom to stand, and as she ventures forth into traffic I go with her. My feet dance uncertainly alongside her, but I embrace it. All is well, and we reach the bank across the road.

Past the Barclay's bank, the *daladala* are gathered. As usual, conductors are repeating destinations in rapid strings of sound *Bu-bu-bu-Bu-bu-bu-Bu-bu-bu!* I keep in step with my new, brave companion.

FRIDAY MORNING

U-wa-nja-wa-nde-geee-U-wa-nja-wa-ndegeee! My companion turns eastward into Vikokotoni's sprawling shortcuts. *To-mo-ndo-To-mo-ndo-To-mo-ndooo!* No matter, I know the way on my own. *Kwe-re-kwe-Kwe-re-kwe-Jamani-Kwe-oh—* this last one blindly flourishes his wrist and it lands a blow right on my shoulder.

"Oh! Careful now. *Kwe-re-kweee!*"

My hand somberly rubs the throbbing part of my shoulder where the careless *konda* has struck me. Weaving between two buses where they have left a narrow space to pass I choose to forget about this small accident. It was only that—an accident. That man did not intend to hit me, and it does not really hurt. Today, I am above small accidents and little pains.

Reassuring my shoulder that it is going to be fine, I reach that familiar entrance to Vikokotoni. There, somehow an eager salesman is still promoting his thick bath towels. Silently, I wish him the best, but I cannot be distracted with his business.

While my eyes passively take in the surroundings, I pick up on a different energy. While Kikwajuni and the Gardens have been quiet today, the space here seems to hum. It is more quiet than usual, yes, but chattering permeates the air. Whispering surrounds me. Generally, it seems that everyone is either moving away from Vikokotoni or into it.

A pattern is forming, too, I think. Mostly ladies move away from Vikokotoni, and mostly men migrate into those narrow passageways. Ladies clutching baskets in hands cross the road into Darajani. Others, balancing bundles on heads, step quickly into buses. Clusters of men dressed in their formal, floor-length *kanzu* gowns pass on either side of me. Peeking through their hems, brown sandals move along with haste. Clearly steered toward Friday prayer, the men direct themselves into Vikokotoni.

The *mwadhana* announces the call to prayer: *Allaaaaahu-akbar-Allahu-akbarrr.* This one, it comes from the speakers attached to the minaret of Ijumaa Mosque. I know this because I recognize this caller's distinct sound. A little aged, a hoarseness is discernible through his strong, professional voice.

While the *mwadhana* is performing his call, I stand patiently here next to a display of leather shoes. My body is accustomed not to moving about while the prayer caller sings. If we eat, handfuls of rice ready to reach lips, we wait. Usually, Auntie puts the television on mute if we watch it. Traditional gentlemen halt their conversations mid-sentence until the *mwadhana* has finished.

After *la-ilaha-illaaa-Allaaaah*, the minaret's loud speakers audibly switch off. In the sudden absence of sacred sound, silence remains for just a moment. Then, the unmistakable humming recommences. Market-going ladies move with a little more quickness than seems normal. The man who sells bath towels, he alternates between glancing at Ijumaa Mosque and listening to the phone pressed to his ear. I am aware of an unusual energy. It makes me feel that there is some collective understanding which has not been shared yet with me.

All of this buzzing energy has me inspired. I wish to record it. Today, I flit carefree through the streets, but a girl can flit just as well with a notepad in hand. Indeed, my present-focused mind is especially well suited for careful observation today.

Notepad withdrawn, my feet turn toward the Darajani side of Haile Selassie Road. My eyes observe an unusual scene. Nearly a dozen soldiers in their uniforms colored like dying leaves stand across from me. They cradle rifles in one hand. A few chat amongst each other, but most peer around themselves. Unlike the security boy of the boys who make plans, these eyes are more of a hawk's. They are not quite aggravated and beady like a hippo's. It is as if they expect something to happen at any moment.

Actually, the way that they watch the ones around them reminds me strangely of myself. I imagine that the way their eyes are now is quite like the way mine are when I carefully watch the ones I see and record notes about them.

Gleefully, I wonder if these uniformed men might be worth watching. Recording notes on these ones who clearly make mental notes of the ones around them—that is amusing. My mind is formulating a title for Page 26 while my feet carry us across Haile Selassie Road.

Pausing briefly, I find shelter beside an Indian man's round belly as a *daladala* barrels dangerously in front of us, headed south toward the airport road. The Indian man, another young woman, and me, we form a little island in the middle of the road. A shining, red motorbike speeds past our backs. It is followed by two taxis. We must wait here in the middle, though, until the buses and taxis in front of us give way to an interlude during which our island might rejoin the mainland in Darajani.

Finally, the rotund Indian man places a foot forward. A pause just long enough for our passage is presenting itself. A version of me more preoccupied with caution might hesitate, but it is a carefree version of me that walks now. I am unafraid. And, the size of this Indian man's belly is not unhelpful since it blocks view of oncoming traffic.

As we reach the other side, the man scratches at his white beard and leaves my side. He wanders toward the date sellers. The young woman ventures in the other direction toward the spice market. It is my duty to join her after all, but I am too intrigued by these stoic officers. Anyway, Auntie has requested spices for next week's *pilau*. Is there really a rush to have them today? I do not think so.

My mind has settled on a title for Page 26. My fingers slide open the cover and turn to the next blank page. My left hand folds Page 25 away from sight. However, pencil does not make it to paper because suddenly, I am distracted.

Kah-kah! I am distracted by a loud noise coming from behind me. A sound like a wooden board clapping against concrete in a big, open space echoes throughout the market.

All at once, many things are happening as a result of this sound. The officers around me here grip their rifles more firmly. All of them race across the road into Vikokotoni on the other side, and one of them is speaking very quickly into an intimidatingly large handheld radio. Their boots hammer the paved road with oppressive thuds, *duh-duh-duh.*

At the same time, a dozen crows are lifting up into the sky over the marketplace. Shrieking hatefully, they flee. I tell you, there is an observable difference between an animal which moves and one which flees. These ones, I know that they are distressed. They are not flying for dinner, but rather for survival. The raucous birds and the diligent soldiers are the first to move, and they do so with efficient purpose.

Just a moment after them, ordinary people like me start to react. The ones nearest here who have seen the uniformed men stomp across the road experience sudden changes in facial expression. Some youthful men appear nervously excited, and they stand firmly watching Vikokotoni. A few of them even follow after the soldiers. Many simply are looking confused. Me, I am probably one among this group. Others, they are looking frightened, and those ones do not stay for long. Ladies pull their children toward the safety of Stonetown's alleys. Elderly men let out distraught sighs before turning and slowly marching away from the scene.

This is something unusual indeed! Too much action is all taking place so quickly, though, that my pencil cannot properly connect to paper.

Then, the noise again pierces the uneasy atmosphere, *kah! kah-kah!* It repeats itself a few more times *kah-kah-kah!* Like hands beating a snare drum, but magnified and echoing all around us, it sounds.

This time, many more people are pouring out of Vikokotoni into the road. The first to emerge and flee south toward the *daladala* buses are women and a few young men. In their faces, I can see confusion. Many mouths are open in startled panic. Elderly men in *kanzu* and *kofia* follow them. They have been at Friday prayer, but something terrible has interrupted them.

All the while, some men rush in the opposite way. Some of these ones are carrying things like stones or bottles. A few of them carry sticks. What is this? I know that I have nothing to fear, but I do become worried. For the first time, my carefree nature is challenged.

"—*Msikiti Ijumaa*," a woman says behind me to a lady in *niqabu*.

"So many gathered there to mourn," she continues, "but the army warned them."

My feet bring me closer to these ladies.

"What have they done?" I ask. "Why has the army warned them, what does it mean, this?"

They both turn to me. I think they are surprised to see a young girl engaging with them right now.

Confirming my thoughts, the one retorts, "*Mwanangu*, what are you doing here? You should just go home now!"

"What has happened?" I insist.

The other whispers through her *niqab*, "Ijumaa Mosque, child. Hundreds have gone there for prayer. They wanted to mourn the ones who died in the accident, *ya Allah*—"

"—But they were too many," the first lady cuts in, "and they are at Ijumaa Mosque."

My eyes look at them quizzically.

"*Msikiti Ijumaa*, it is the favorite place for *Uamsho*," the second lady fervently whispers.

The things that Bwana Usi has always said must be true, then.

"They were mourning—" I start.

"Yes, but the union police do not care, child. They do not see mourners. They see hundreds of protestors: *wauamsho*. They cannot have them gathered all together."

Kah!

The lady in *niqab* takes the other's hand in her own, and she directs them away from the market. Turning, I position myself to view the other side. Vikokotoni is a storm of activity. *Kah-kah!* I hear its thunder. Some kind of lightning flashes across the storefronts.

Now, some of those young men with stones and sticks come racing back out of the alleyways. One bumps into the bath towel salesman, who is throwing tarps over his wares. His escape has come too late, though, as several more youth crash into him. His stacks are toppling. He shouts at them angrily, but seems to admit defeat: he flees across the road toward me.

Close behind the young, armed men, the union soldiers reemerge. I understand the lightning flashes now. *Kah-kah!* Their rifles unload bright blasts. One of the young men yells in pain, a big nasty bruise visible under a fresh tear in his football jersey.

This area does not feel so safe, I concede. Though I am free and unafraid today, I am not wanting tears or bruises. Anyway, hibiscus and spices can wait. Dauda has insisted that today is a more convenient time to go to market. This may have been true, but clearly things are changing.

Swiftly, I take the path laid out by those ladies. I am small, so I am able to slide between others who hesitate and block the way. Turning sideways, I step between a very round lady and an elderly man who has dropped his bag of chickens. The birds' legs are tied, so they are not escaping. Still, their commotion is enough to startle everyone who is already quite startled.

Nimbly, my feet step over a grumpy chicken who has flopped some feet away from his owner. I continue. Me, I am not panicked like some around me. I am more captivated by the intrigue. All along the road, people have suddenly abandoned whatever it is that they have been doing.

Passing the corner cafe, I see piles of unopened coconuts. The seller is absent. Oh! He has just taken off without even covering them. Farther down, the Italian restaurant has shuttered all of their windows. These ones, they like to be separated behind their well-groomed shrubs, but at least their windows are usually open. Of course, people racing haphazardly across Haile Selassie Road is not typical, either. With disregard for the few cars which speed away from the market, people fling themselves this way and that.

Today is truly unusual in all of these ways. Obviously, union soldiers do not usually act this way. I suppose that hundreds of mourners do not usually gather at one mosque, either. Who truly to blame for the disruption, then, is eluding me. Really, the ferry boat accident is the most at fault. That accident is the reason for all of the noise and all of the pain.

With these thoughts on my mind, my feet take a pause from fleeing. They have reached the end of Haile Selassie, near the place where I have taken Page 23's notes about those boys who make plans.

Now, the small store that sells soaps and fried sweets is boarded up like the Italian restaurant. The man who sells oranges and tangerines is also not here. All the same, I take a seat on the small stoop. To my side, a few things hang from the store awning. Brightly colored bags of tomato-flavored crisps sway as people rush past them.

Finally, I am far enough from the hubbub to safely take some notes about this peculiar scene. Pencil touches to Page 26. I direct my eyes up the road to do some investigation.

Immediately they are overwhelmed with sights. Ladies who have been in the thick of shopping are now in the heat of running. They trip over the apples they spill from their own woven baskets. Learners who have been putting the last touches on their exams are emerging from Haile Selassie with astonished eyes and wide open mouths. Some of them, I tell you, are thrilled by the chaos, and they hesitate only a moment before dashing down the road toward the market. I hope that their curiosity does not bring them harm, *inshaallah*.

Kah-kah! Hurrying toward me, men of all ages have come from mosque. At the corner, they turn either into Stonetown or toward the airport road. You see, most people flee the scene. Most people desperately get away from the soldiers and their bruising bullets—but not all people.

Finally, I see what must be inspiring the soldiers' furious reaction. A group of young men has come into view. I recognize a few of them from those ones who have gone running into Vikokotoni with bottles and stones in their fists. These men are holding a big, white banner. Painted in black letters, something is written on the side facing the union officers. There are red designs, too—that is unpleasant; too much like blood.

I worry that the red paint is not going to be the only blood on Haile Selassie Road before this has returned to calm. But, do not worry about me. I am safe here on this stoop behind the store and its crisps swinging in the commotion. Today, I am free like a flying fish. I nimbly flit through waves—dangerous ones and calm ones, all the same. Do not worry about me.

Me, I worry about these bold men and their banner. What is worth exposing themselves to rifle fire like this? What has angered the soldiers opposing them?

Kah! Kah! A young man, head covered by a nice, brown *kofia*, he stumbles and falls. I think he has been hit by one of the bullets. His hands press against the paved road, but he cannot return to his feet. As he struggles, the muscles in his wide shoulders bulge. I see his face. His skin is dark, and he has a wide, flat nose. I know him! This is the *chairman* of those boys who make plans. This is *Yusuf*. My fingers search for his story in my notes, Page 21—no, no—Page— but, my eyes cannot look away.

Kah! An older man in a long *kanzu* the color of cream is hit by the rifle's lightning. He yelps in brief agony, and he falls to the ground. Without his support, the banner crookedly flops.

Another man takes his place and straightens it, but for the short moment between I can see what the banner proclaims. Written in the thick, black letters is JUMUIYA YA UAMSHO—ZENJI NCHI YETU!—WAZANZIBAR WAAMKE!—MUUNGANO UFUTWE! That is, *'The Association for Uamsho—Zenji is our nation—Zanzibaris wake up!—End the Union!'*

These are *wauamsho*. All along, that sneaking committee meeting—it is as I suspected. I must add to the notes I have taken. This unusual story has certainly grown.

"*Takbiiiiiir!*" Someone cries.

"*Allahu akbar! Allahu akbar!*" the angry *wauamsho* marching in the road reply, "*Allahu akbar! Zenji ni nchi yetu! Uamshooo!*"

Suddenly, three massive cars are speeding past me. In shock, I nearly fall right off my stoop.

"*Hebu* look at thaaaat one!" a young boy proclaims delightedly, pointing at the monstrous vehicles. His sister takes hold of the pointing hand and drags him urgently toward Kikwajuni.

Kah! Kah-kah!

Allahu akbar! Zenji nchi yetu!

These cars are more like tanks than taxis. Their color is the military green color of rotten avocadoes. All of their edges are squared, like a box. Atop each of them, five or six soldiers stand with more rifles. Other heavy, round pieces of machinery are with them, too.

Kah!

—nchi yetu!

As the colossal, boxy tanks get closer to the market, a new noise joins the shouting.

Duuuunh!

It is similar to the *kah!* of the rifles, but more like a bass drum than a snare. This noise prompts a different kind of reaction, too. A moment after I hear it, several men appear, running in the opposite direction. One of them has a cloth pressed to his face. Oh, what has happened now?

My feet bring me to standing. My carefree nature is shaken, I admit it.

Soon, I have my answer to this question. A smoke is following after these men, caught in the sea breeze and billowing like a little cloud. This cloud is a very strange one. It is the color of an ordinary, calm cloud, but of course it is here on the ground. It seems to have come from the military car.

Now, it extends up and up into the sky and out into the demonstrators. They, in turn, cry out and cover their faces. What kind of funny cloud is this that makes big men suddenly cry? This makes me nervous and my feet dig anxiously into the sandy pavement.

Doubt creeps into my thoughts and I question my being here. An itching anxiety scratches at my sides. Whispers start to warn me that I have made grave mistakes.

Kah-kah! Kah!

Duuuunh!

My heart starts to beat too quickly.

As I pivot to turn on my left foot, I am hit by a heavy thing. It knocks me flat onto the paved road. *Oh!* My notepad leaves my pocket and flops haphazardly toward the crying cloud, which has grown even bigger now.

Adjusting my headscarf, I look up to examine what heavy thing rudely hit me so. My heart beats faster still. This heavy thing is a body belonging to a boy, and he does not look at all sorry to have knocked me down.

"*Mtundu*, stupid girl, what are you doing here?"

I disregard him as I can tell his words are not meant for kind conversation. My notepad needs my help more than he does, I am sure. I lift myself carefully. Nothing is broken, but my ankle pains me a little. Oh, this boy is the stupid one—so reckless.

He has taken notice of my notepad and swiftly reaches it before I am able.

"*Ndo nini*? But really, what are you doing here, you?…I've seen you. You are this girl who is always writing things. It is like you are in school all the time."

At first, I bristle because as we both know, I am not like a learner taking notes in a lecture. No, I am like a detective, carefully looking and observing the truth. Nonetheless, my face drains of warmth and fills with dread. Has he really seen me taking notes before?

Then, I recognize him. This is another of those boys who makes plans from Page 23—that is it, of course I remember now. As my heart races, I think still, I must add to those pages once I am safely home, after-the-fact.

Yes, he is the one who shaves his head clean bald. This is the security, that one who shoved me with his stupid, hippo eyes. He is the one whose forehead wrinkles when he listens. Well, his forehead is wrinkly even now, so perhaps this is really, truly just the way he looks.

"Oh! *Hellooo!*" He waves my notepad up and down to regain my full attention.

Kah!

Ya Allaaaah!

"Get out of your little book," he spits, "everyone is doing something and just you are writing! Do not write, *mtundu*—listen!"

My fingers wriggle with desire to snatch the notepad from his outstretched hand, but his hand jerks backward, toward the cloud and the crowd.

"Can't you hear? Can't you hear what they are saying? Can't you read the banner?"

He smiles in a way that is nasty and reminds me of a way Fahadi's father would smile sometimes. Sometimes, I would gain sudden courage enough to tell him to leave our mother alone, not to touch her anymore. We both would be surprised by my outburst. Then, his smile—this smile, it would appear and I would be silent again.

Kah!

I tell you, this smile is a dirty trick which men play. It is not a '*you have made me happy*' smile, but more an '*I know a thing which you can never know*' type of smile. This smile may cause you to think they have heard you or are with you, but their eyes and their lips conspire to give you a clue; a clue that they do not hear you and that they are not with you. No, they are with themselves and once the moment passes, we girls return to being alone and unheard.

Thus, though I demand my little notepad with all firmness of which I am capable, "*Nipe basi!*" I am not heard.

The moment—along with the nasty smile—pass. His lips return to a serious frown and his hands, oh, his hands, *jamani*, they tear my notepad from end to end.

"Read the banner, *we!*" he tears the pages, "*Uamsho!*" he tears the binding, "Wake up!"

He casts halves of pages onto the road and into the burning, crying cloud.

Duuuunh! Kah-kah-kah!

"Stupid girl, it doesn't matter! Your schooling, your chores, your future! It's nothing without our freedom—wake up!"

The burning cloud is at its biggest, and it wraps around me and the terrible boy who makes plans just as he tosses the notepad's broken spine to his feet. A sharp pain, like a thousand red chilies and a hundred January suns greets my eyes and my skin.

Sorrow for my beloved notepad is suddenly overshadowed by pain. Pain in my heart is giving way to pain in my eyes, my throat, my chest, and my fingers.

The boy has fled. In front of me, scraps of paper are rolling about the road—those are the observations I have collected. Those scraps are the many stories I have preserved. Each page is a person. One of those pages is the very same boy who destroyed them all.

My eyes burn intensely. They fill with tears, and my nose flows with hot liquid. Crying has never hurt like this. Even in that night of wailing on Kiwimbi, when Bi. Mwinyi shook my shoulders and led me home—crying has not hurt like this.

Oh, what is happening? Sorrow surely grips me, but this burning cloud rips at me. The air hijacks my sorrow.

In a moment of blurred vision, I look for whole pages. My body drops to its knees, and I scavenge—my fingers like chickens picking at sandy pavement. They pluck desperately at the ground for scraps of paper pages like hungry beaks searching for bugs. But, my eyes, they can barely stay open for even a moment. I cannot see through mucus and tears. My fingers, too, start to burn and searching the ground is irritating my skin. It cannot go on. I rise to my feet and cough deeply, painfully.

With wild urgency, I command my feet to move us. I must leave this place.

My feet begin to run.

I begin to run.

I run from *Uamsho* and the union police. I run from the burning cloud. I run into the gardens, coughing and sputtering. I tell you, I know only that I reach Jamhuri Gardens by the fact that my feet brush thick grass. Some sort of leafy plants cushion me as I tumble downward and spit up more burning mucus.

A scream boils up from my fiery lungs. It reaches my teeth, which are clenched shut. I release them. I release it. I scream.

I howl into the gardens. The howling becomes a wail. The wailing becomes a cry. I am unsure if the tears sliding across my cheeks and off the tip of my nose are from the burning gases or from the pain in my belly.

Duuuunh!

The pain I have felt in some way small or large since my mother vanished months ago is as clear as blue sky to me now. The hollow feeling which haunts me has a name. It is grief. It is desperate, longing grief.

Too much to handle, I cough up the feeling. I literally wretch it up and spit it out. It escapes through my eyes in itchy streams. I do not want it anymore. I cannot hold it.

Allahu akbar!

Trying to be like Dauda and busy myself with productive tasks has not healed me. Trying to be like Fahad, avoiding the past and living moment to moment, has not given me reprieve. It has remained in me, and I think it will stay with me.

No, let me be rid of it. Let me let go of it. I cannot silently hold this grief. I want to survive. I want my body—and my spirit! I want them back, mine. I tire and I suffer from neglecting one for the other, and now neither belong to me.

"*Mamangu*," I breathe life into her name.

Allahu akbar!

I call upon her spirit without fear.

When I cry for her—for her memory—I feel that it is real, at least. Because it hurts, I know that it is still here. Though the memory is painful, I know that it exists. It is real. It is a truth.

Resolving to be strong has left me weakened. Avoiding, neglecting, distracting, they have transformed me into a skittish version of the girl I have known myself to be.

I cough up a spirit that has taken up residence in me while I have been away.

Kah-kah!

Heaving up phlegm, I spit it into the bushes. With this, I also release a thing that does not belong in me. More importantly, I do not belong to it. Some twisted thing born from grief and pain that I no longer wish to carry—I hurl it up and spit it out.

I do not want it. I refuse it. And, I do not fear it. I give it a name. I am whole—broken but whole. *Ya Allah*, let my spirit be the only in me. Let my sorrow out to sea. Fill me up with your serenity, *ya Allah*, the Light. Let it overflow, let it be as intense as it must be, like a spark that hurts. It burns, it leaves a mark. It is pain, but it is brightness in the dark…like love…like a memory of love.

Ya Allah!

Tears continue to stream down my face, but I find my breath returning to me. These tears who remain are not caused by burning gas. These ones, they are for my mother. A pent-up sadness releases more naturally now. The howling and wailing has been as if our water tank at home burst and its contents spilled all at once—a disaster. However, the contents have been poison all along. Now, it is like a cloth has been applied to the opening. Poisons are permitted to exit, but they do so at a more manageable rate.

I wipe fluids from my face. My eyes burn, but vision returns to them. I can see the chaos on Haile Selassie, but I am safely distanced. I can see where it is that I am. I have collapsed into a thicket of soft, flat leaves.

Despite blinded, burning eyes I have made it halfway across Jamhuri. Its playground stands unbothered by soldiers and angry, young men. Certainly, no children play here now and no couples discreetly touch fingertips on benches. The playground is completely empty, in fact.

Kah!

Closest to me, just over the sagging wire fence, stands a slide. It is tall enough for very small ones to enjoy, but it is not meant for me. Painted onto its side—though peeling from age and salty air—are pretty colors of blue sky and blue sea. It bears an ocean scene. In between the frothy waves, dolphins and flying fish frolic. What is this? *Masha'allah,* my creator, He mocks me. Through watery eyes and slimy nostrils, I laugh. I find my chest trembling with joy at the blatant sign here and now beside me.

This slide, it is too small for me. No matter, I lift myself up. I sneeze a great, tickling sneeze. Then, I approach the painted structure. I touch the fish with my right hand. I prod at the painted waves. Who has put these ones here? Have we been on this slide before when we were young, with Fahad and Dauda? Did our mother perch us here and giggle with us as we rode down the smooth metal, painted like the sea? I cannot recall it.

But, that is alright. There are many memories I cannot recall. If they deem me worthy to return one day, I am ready for them—but slowly. They are difficult, memories. They can be like accidents. Suddenly, a boat full of memories can topple over and spill them into an unprepared mind. It is too much.

Duuunh!

In the background, I can hear the noises of Haile Selassie have not calmed. Another loud one expands the poisonous smoke. Rifles unload into furious boys who had made plans *kah-ka-kaah*! It is a mess that should not be. It is an unrighteous response to a wicked accident.

I suppose some people protect themselves by being like the waves. Their strict routine is guidance. Their patterned life keeps them on track and accidents do not affect them except for a brief moment when it ripples their current. Others, they are like these flying fish my fingers are touching here. They avoid accidents altogether by their flight. They live with us, but they navigate with a different set of rules only they understand.

Me, I am not like the waves or the fish. I am not driftwood, either. Me, I am just a girl. I do not belong in the sea. I am not waves, or fish, or even a sailor. I belong here, on land.

With my fingers, I trace the lines of the painted waves, and I laugh again. It is a relief. It is an unburdening. With its predictable waves, the sea has its usual patterns, but it causes accidents, too. Ocean waves are not perfect things. It is just their nature, and it is not their fault. On dark days, they rise and fall unnaturally. On those days, they can even take away mothers.

They took her to be at Allah's side.

With a sputtering cough, I spit into the brush a last time. I exhale. Firmly adjusting my headscarf, I breathe in. I am very tired.

I want to go home.

SATURDAY MORNING

TODAY, RAMADHAN HAS BEGUN. WE have been told that the narrowest sliver of moon has been made visible to us in the night.

This morning, the sun is later to rising. We are close to the equator on Unguja, and so our supply of sunlight is nearly equal all year long. You know this. But, our island lies just south of the equator and this means that July is a little darker than other months. Thus, the sun sleepily creeps inch by inch closer to the horizon some 10 or 15 minutes late. When I arrive to school 15 minutes later, I am reprimanded. Is there no such scolding for the sun? Surely, my lateness is not as impactful as the sun's.

Unguja is also quite flat. I have not yet told you that. There are no mountains for the morning sun to climb. Just, there are some tall trees and small slopes. Even so, the island sun is a lazy one in the morning time. So, those slopes are enough to delay it. Rays of light peek out over the airport road and the blockish towers of Michenzani. This morning sun is like a reluctant spark. It has all the power to light a great, glowing fire. But, we must be patient. We cannot prod it or overwhelm it with our own personal demands. Like most things here, it comes on its own time, but it will come.

On Unguja, we call this dark but hopeful time *alfajiri*. At this time, many islanders are immersed in prayer. Others, they make their ways to offices, markets, ports. Others still, they come here to Kiwimbi. They join together in groups and they do their daily exercise routines. Travelers are less visible at *alfajiri*. I imagine that they are comfortably asleep in airconditioned hotel rooms. I do not know the names of those places. They have not told me, but I have never asked them.

Me, I sit here alone. Asha and Khadija have likely also woken up already, but it is not our habit to meet at sunrise. It is during evenings after schoolwork has finished that we tend to sit here together. I know that Dauda has seen me go out, since I have given her a sturdy shove while exiting the bed. The shove, it is not intentional, but I am a clumsy girl in the morning.

Since she has seen me, I do not preoccupy myself with wondering if Auntie worries for me at home. I have come early to Kiwimbi before. It is not something she has deemed worthy of shouting or beating. Today is Ramadhan. I doubt she will change her precedent now of all days. Now is a time for focused patience and purposeful forgiveness.

Taking a lesson from clever Asha, I have located a stray leaf of newspaper. It becomes my seat, protecting my bottom from cool sand. The sand nearly feels damp this morning. It might have rained a little last night. That would be good. Rain brings blessings. It brings life. It is needed, especially now. Let it bless this Holy Month and bring us renewal.

As I slide into a comfortable position on my copy of *Zanzibar Leo*, I spy a pen in the sand. Someone must have dropped it here. It is not mine, is it? No, the night of the boat accident, my notepad was still safely in my hands along with its partner pen. This one here, it is from some other clumsy writer. I pick it up, and brush grit off its tip. Testing it on my thumb, I see that it still works.

"Ah, here you are," a voice says to my right side.

I look up, expecting to see a boy from Haile Selassie Secondary School or from Michenzani, perhaps sent by Khadija to relay me some message—meet her in Jamhuri or somewhere farther down the beach.

I look up, and instead of a boy like that I see the *mzungu*, the one who runs. I think he reads the surprise in my eyes, because he adjusts his posture to appear less threatening.

His right hand placed on his chest, he says, "Sorry! I have startled you."

These words he uses, they are truly Swahili of Unguja. His government has done a proper job of his education, this one.

"Are you well? How is your day? I was looking for you, sister."

He does not even give me time to reply, oh. Here, his selfish, foreign attitude shows through his polished, local accent.

"Yesterday, I was at the library—you know it, the one across from Jamhuri there. I saw you there when the gas bombs went off."

My heart sinks a little into my belly. The rawness in my throat has not fully subsided, and knowing that he was there, too, it is embarrassing. My cheeks feel warm with shame.

"I am so sorry," he says; *pole*, it is the 'sorry' full of empathy. Foreigners do not have this expression. At least, that is what Auntie tells me. She says that Europeans have 'sorry' for *excuse me* or *forgive me*, or even *please say that again*. But, they do not have this one—'*pole*' for *I feel for your pain*.

"Thank you," I reply. My heart rises a little bit toward its correct place in my chest. I appreciate his sentiment.

"*Tena pole sana*. And, I saw what happened, sister. I saw that one who took your journal. That was a shame and a disgrace. What evil people!"

"Thank you."

"Yes. *Pole, dada*. So, I have been looking for you now."

I find myself still suspect of this moment and this behavior. I draw my scarf closer to my cheeks.

"Saturdays, I do not have classes, so I have time to go to the market. There, I bought an extra book—a notebook. I have another one for me, so if you want, *dadangu*, you may take this one."

He extends his hands and shows a small book to me. It is not unlike my old one, with its wire-bound spine and its lined pages. Its cover, though, is not a dark blue color of deep waters. This one, its cover is a color like magnolia flowers or watermelon candy. This one, it is pink like a 10-thousand-shilling bill. It is a nice color, truly.

However, my feelings are mixed.

"You should not have bought me things. I do not know you"

"No, no, sister, I bought books for myself. I have an extra one and I saw yesterday what happened to you—that is way I come to you with it now. I have one more than needed and I think you have one less."

Auntie likes to remind me that in Islam when we give and we do so with Allah in mind, then He will multiply our blessings. When clouds give rain to farmers, the farmers are blessed with corn, cassava, and potatoes. The Qur'an tells us that those farmers ought to give one part of their harvest to charity, one part they feed their families, and the last part they use to replant for next year's harvest. This is how Allah multiplies what we have when we share it generously. When we share without expectations, we are blessed again and again. No one need to be without.

This *mzungu*, maybe he is Muslim. My old notepad, its pages would tell you that he has an Arab father. But, that notepad is gone now, and here is the *mzungu* who runs offering me a replacement. His story lives on without the story I have written him.

When he shares, does he share without expectations? What does he want from me in return—or does he truly share a part of his bounty, knowing that his blessing comes later? Many *wazungu*, when they share they expect something in return.

They hold stakes—no, no, what is it—they call themselves 'stakeholders,' and they call their gifts 'investments.' They consider risks and benefits. This *mzungu*, it is clear to me that his Swahili comes from his own country's investment in him. They hold a stake in his knowledge, and his return with gained expertise will prove their investment a wise one full of many benefits and few risks. This is the system he knows. This sort of system does not align with what Auntie has taught me. When she cites the Holy Book, she makes no mention of stakeholders or investments. She cites blessed rain and unconditional giving.

"What do you want from me?"

"Sorry?"

This time, it is not *I feel for your pain* but *please say that again*.

"What do you want me to do with your book?"

He hesitates before speaking. He is youthful and does not have many wrinkles, but there are little ones just above his eyebrows. These wrinkles are visible now as he considers my question.

Then he simply says, "No."

"Enh?"

"No, *dadangu*, I want nothing at all." His voice is solemn. He speaks deliberately. "What those angry men did was wrong. Your book was not theirs to take, to ruin. I have another one. That is all."

We lock eyes and hold a moment's silence.

"Do you want it?"

His right heel lifts and he rocks onto his toes. I think he means to leave me very soon.

"*Haya … haya*, yes, I want it."

His heel comes back to the sandy ground. He extends his right hand again and offers me the pink-colored notepad.

"*Nashukuru*," I thank him.

"God bless you," I add.

He nods and smiles. Perhaps he does indeed require nothing else.

Still, I cannot help but think that most *wazungu* are the same, even if they seem to be unusual like this one. One day in the future, he might find me again and ask me what I have done with his gift. He might ask to know what I have written in his investment. Does he feel that he holds a stake in me now? I should hope not.

Nevertheless, I am glad to have a notepad here in my hands. A gift is a gift. *Zawadi ni tunda la moyo*, it is said; 'a gift is fruit from the heart.' I accept it with gratitude, and may Allah multiply the blessings of the *mzungu* who runs.

As for the *mzungu*, he murmurs one more '*haya*' and when I look up again, he has gone. At a calm pace, he is walking to the side of the airport road and waits for a safe moment to cross. On his feet, he still wears those nice running shoes. I can spot them, even from this far, because their silver color glistens in the early morning sunshine. However, it does seem that their white and sapphire colors have faded—perhaps from the dust of a week's exercises. This one, either he must not have someone polishing his shoes for him or he has indeed been in Africa for a time now. Though, if he has been here for a while, then he ought to know that one will not get any respect with dirty footwear. He must spend less time purchasing extra books and more time making himself presentable.

Anyway, it is not the shoes that I hold now in my hands. Here, cradled in my lap I hold a new notepad. My fingers hesitate to lift its pink cover, but I urge them on. A gift is a gift. Now, my instinct is to return home. In the safety of the courtyard, I might write another story. I might write about the *mzungu who runs and gives gifts*. I might write about *the boys who make plans to start riots*. You see, there is much to add to the stories I have thought I was knowing.

However, home can be a busy place in the morning. Dauda will insist I help her move the mattress away. Auntie will interrogate me about having gone out so early. Fahadi will cry because he does not want to wake, and he will pout because he does not want Ramadhan to start. He will let a cat loose in the courtyard, Dauda will shout at him, and Auntie will threaten to spank his bottom. Washing will be overdue, and beans will need to be soaked—but not eaten until we break the fast after *magharibi*. There, I will have no time for writing.

I grip the slender, blue pen firmly in my hand and I touch its tip to the paper as I have done so many times before. But, this time is different. This time is different because I do not write other people's stories based on looking carefully and observing. I do not make any good guesses about others. No, this time I make no guesses at all, though I do look carefully.

I look carefully inward at myself—at Tatu, a girl from Unguja, from Kikwajuni, near Sheikh Kareem Mosque, near a beach named Kiwimbi.

This time is different because I write for me, not for you.

Owh, but you may stay if you like.

PAGE 1

MY NAME IS TATU KHAMIS Mohamad Abdullah Mustafa Abdullah al-Habsi. I am a girl who lives on Unguja, the biggest island in Zanzibar. Here, I live with my auntie, my sister, and my little brother. My sister is Dauda Gharib Salim Mohammed Sayed Idd al-Aziz. My little brother is Fahad Boon Teong. Our older brother lives in Dar es Salaam, but we do not see him often. The ferry ride to Dar is expensive, and the waves nauseate us much more often than they comfort us. Our brother is Khalid Gharib Salim Mohammed Sayed Idd al-Aziz. My auntie, she is our mother's eldest sister. I do not know all seven of her names. She has never told me. At least, she has told me but sometimes it changes, and so I am unsure what is the truth. She herself might be unsure. She is simply Mama Nuru. Her eldest child, Nuru, is our cousin, born just a few months after Dauda.

Dauda and me, we have lived with Auntie ever since our mother disappeared. Fahadi joined us after some weeks of sojourning from place to place. He went first to our uncle in Bububu. Then, he came back to Kikwajuni, and stayed with Usi, Mzee Ameir's son. I remember the bad day when Bwana Usi thought Fahadi was with Auntie and Auntie knew him to be with Usi. Truly, he was in neither place, but all other places: wandering around neighborhoods, playing with chickens.

After that day, Auntie insisted Fahad come to stay with us. Auntie is more adept at discipline than Usi or Mzee Ameir. At first, Auntie practiced this discipline often since Fahadi frustrates her with his large personality and stubbornness. After months of minimal results, she has eased. As long as he is not wandering alone, dancing and playing with dirty animals; as long as he is naughty at home rather than naughty out in some place wherever, Auntie accepts this. I am happy Fahadi stays with us. He frustrates me, too, but he is my brother. He needs me.

I need him, too. While Fahadi's eyes remind me of his father who was not kind, his dancing and laughing reminds me of our mother. More than Dauda or me, Fahadi inherited our mother's joy.

Our mother was a good lady. She is not here with us, but she is present in my life and in my story. She is the reason for who, why, where, how, and what I am. We loved her, but Allah loves her more, and so he took her. This is what Bi. Mwinyi tells me. I believe her.

Our mother was a black, African woman. Her skin was light. It was lighter than mine, but her eyes were darker than my own. Under her eyes and on her forehead she had a few little black spots on her skin. Dauda and I gave names to those spots, and we spent whole afternoons laughing about it. We shook with laughter when I named the one on her left cheek Jamila, and we trembled uncontrollably when Dauda named the biggest one on her forehead Barack Obama.

Our mother was always moving. She moved to and from the clothing markets in Vikokotoni, to and from the shops in Shangani, and the bank in Kiswandui. We always had enough money thanks to her perpetual motion. I am not sure what she was selling in these places. Now, it is too late to ask. We do not speak about the ones who have left us.

Our mother's hair was usually a little unkempt. Only the ones at home, we knew this, because she wrapped it tightly in *kanga* or silky headscarves the moment she set her feet to public spaces. Mama was the one who taught me not to go around with my naked hair. She taught me how to wrap a headscarf very quickly. She never wore *niqabu*, though, unlike Auntie. I do not know why, and now it is too late to ask.

When her hair was not covered, it stuck out at angles. Some parts were brushed smooth like dense cotton, but always some parts rebelled and protruded this way and that. Auntie often braided it for her, taming it nicely. She liked to wear it in tight, straight braids close to her scalp. But, she was having Auntie do this for her and never the salon ladies. I am not ten-out-of-ten certain why, but I think it was to be at home with us. I think that while other ladies take time to tend to their hair at salons, our mother tended to us.

Her thin arms were much stronger than they looked. With an iron grip, those arms would guide Fahad to where he ought to be. He was never lost while our mother was here. One in each hand, those arms carried overflowing water cans. Dauda never had to work as hard while Mama was here. My shoulders never knew tenseness while our mother was here, because the strength in her hands massaged any hint of tenseness away before it could really start.

Mama was a sharp lady. She gave the best advice. Khalid was born when she was 15 years old, I think, maybe 16, so she was always younger than other parents, but older than Khalid's peers. I think this is why she had a way of understanding all people. The wisdom of elders was hers, but so was the playfulness of youthful people like Dauda and me.

Mama was a funny lady. That lady, she would make people laugh even in the moments most unfit for laughter. That was her gift. Even prickly, old men were taken by surprise at her charms. Bi. Mwinyi and Mzee Ameir spent hours sitting on stoops with our mother. They gossiped and opined. Bi. Mwinyi cackled when our mother teased her for gaining weight. Mzee Ameir laughed deep and slow laughs that made his belly jiggle when our mother dramatically flirted with him. Swahili children, they can be expert teasers and jokesters, but no child was a match for our mother.

I remember when we came home from school—Dauda, Khadija, Asha, and me—with a plan. It was a boring Tuesday in April. It was so very boring, I recall, that we decided to take matters into our own hands and make it less boring. The arrogance it took for us as young girls to believe we might change the nature of time and place, we should have expected a scolding. When days decide to be dull, one lets them be dull. Only Allah can change a day. Anyway, Khadija suggested we play a trick on Fahadi.

Khadija said it would be better to do something about our boredom than to sit around complaining. We agreed. I agreed because I was thinking we might look at the ones who exercise at Kiwimbi, or hunt for the prettiest shells on the beach. These are good ways to change a dull day. Those ways are not so arrogant; they are simple. Khadija had a different idea. Once we had bought into her desire for action, she led us back to our house. Holding my hand in hers, she pulled me along mischievously.

Dauda and Asha followed, carefully avoiding the deepest and darkest puddles. Occasionally, Khadija's momentum carried me through a murky one—*dwuuu!*—and my school shoes suffered for her haste. I can still hear Asha's wicked giggles and Dauda disapprovingly sucking her teeth after each messy splash.

After a few soggy encounters, we crossed Haile Selassie Road and found ourselves in Kikwajuni. Even then, Khadija withheld her master plan. I would have been more peeved with her if I had not also been eager for adventure. It was not until reaching the rusty, red courtyard door that Khadija finally paused.

She called *Hodi! Hodi huku!* No one answered, so we knew that Auntie and our mother were out shopping or visiting some sister's cousin's sister. As this became clear, Khadija smiled a naughty smile. I can see it now. All our faces awaited a response from inside, blank and patient. After a very silent moment, Khadija's tamely patient eyes became little flames. I recognized them from cooking over firewood. Her eyes were the spark that starts the fire. Unlike the useless, little sparks which come before, it is an enduring one—one that will lead to action.

Sawa, she concluded, but announced, *Hodi humo!* one more time for good measure as we entered through the empty courtyard. Hanging from lines, a few *kanga* were dancing gently in the breeze. They were intended to dry in the sun, but that morning provided much more rain than sun. I compared my shoes to the *kanga*. It was unclear which was soggier, which more dissatisfying.

Naam, haya, Khadija said, turning around to face the rest of us in the kitchen. She began to detail her plan at last.

We would first collect our clean uniforms from Dauda's dresser. We would take my most pretty and feminine shoes: the ones a color like green pistachio ice cream. Those are my best shoes; for weddings and *Eid el-Fitr*. Then, we would go to Fahad's room and take his uniform away, hiding it in some place. We would tell him that Mama gave away his clothes to a cousin, and that he must wear a girl's uniform for the rest of the term.

She smacked her hands together triumphantly. He would cry and pout as he always does when he is compared to a little girl, but he would also put on the uniform because he is gullible and naive. He would believe whatever we told him. He would put on the girl's uniform, and become very upset. Fahadi is especially comical when he is upset like this. The result would be a dull day transformed into a very memorable one. We would laugh and laugh and always remember that day when our little brother was so silly for being upset about a stupid lie.

At first, I think, I hesitated. It was a stupid lie, after all. But, Asha giggled and Dauda sucked her teeth disapprovingly, and I think that I wanted to be on the side of giggling and against teeth sucking.

So, we did it. We gathered all the clean uniforms. Of course, Fahadi would only put on one for now. But, for persuasive theatrics, we would present him with all of them. He would be overwhelmed. I would apologize that his own clothes had to be given away—this was Asha's idea—but Dauda would reassure him that he would be alright since we had these girls' clothes for him to keep now—this was my idea. The plan evolved as our excitement grew. Even Dauda succumbed to giggles. Asha impersonated a crying Fahadi. Khadija pranced about the room, channeling naughty anticipation through her feet.

The climactic moment arrived when Fahadi appeared suddenly in the doorway. We had planned to find him in the living room or playing in the street, but oh, this was even better. His interest had already been piqued.

His narrow eyes surveyed all the clothing collected on the bed first. Then, he looked at Asha and Khadija, maybe since they were guests. I was looking at him since I noticed him at the door, and finally when his eyes fell on me I might have hesitated with our plan one more time.

However, Khadija was committed to her innovative fun. Sweeping past me and my sympathetic eyes, she welcomed Fahad in with an arm wrapped around his little shoulders. She reminded him that it was rude to stand in doorways. Then, with his full attention she began to weave the lie.

Everything nicely followed the plan. Khadija explained that our mother and Auntie weren't home because they were giving away Fahadi's clothes. It was charity, *sadaka*. It was a good deed, and not to be questioned. Then, my turn came and I apologized for the inconvenience to him. I comforted him. Finally, Dauda stepped forward and presented all of the girls' items.

I remember Fahadi's eyes, twisted and desperate. Predictably, he began to cry. Asha covered her mouth to hide a smirk. Khadija barely contained giggles. I think I felt some shame, but the amusement and the sense of success for having executed a plan so perfectly overcame this shame. I, too, smiled. I used my smile to further the scheme.

No, no, Fahadi, do not cry, silly one, I reassured him, *we are doing this for you. You have clothes to wear and we who are older will suffer but we will endure it. You do not have to suffer. We will go find clothes. You have some here, and do not have to find any on your own.*

I remember his eyes untwisting a little. He looked at me with trust, but confusion. Fahad is sharp: he knew that my comfort seemed forced and foolish. He knew that he had a right to be upset. Fahad is so expressive—even then. I knew his feelings without exchanging any words.

Suddenly, our plan shifted. Mama and Auntie returned, and our mother entered the room. I think she could sense trouble. She barely glanced at Fahad before demanding, *What have you done to him*?

We balked and halted. We hesitated, but our mother, she is a fierce lady. She drew out the truth like an *mganga* drawing out a bad spirit. Like trickster spirits, Swahili children can be expert teasers and jokesters. No child was a match for our mother.

In short minutes, our mother identified our lie and exposed our conspiracy. She was more efficient than the most unified jury and more commanding than the most intimidating of judges. She looked into our eyes and saw our guilt. She reached a verdict. Our mother, being a clever and very funny lady, she reached a very clever judgment.

As a quiet Auntie and a whimpering Fahadi looked on, Mama gathered up all the girls' clothes from the bed. She bundled them up in her thin, powerful arms. Then, she marched them to the courtyard. We followed nervously. She marched out to Bi. Mwinyi's door and herself hollered *Hodi! Hodi Bibi Mwinyi wee!*

Fearfully from behind the rusty door, we watched as our mother explained how proud she was of her daughters. She told Bi. Mwinyi how we were wanting to donate clothes to *sadaka*, and Mama, she knew that Bi. Mwinyi had been arranging this—so how convenient! How noble and generous, her children, *masha'allah*! *Masha'allah*.

Khadija's eyes connected with my eyes and we both looked at Dauda. Dauda was the first to whimper. A hotness bloomed in my cheeks and I felt that I might start to cry. It was not finished.

Our mother, she then shared a laugh with Bi. Mwinyi. She went on to tell her the other funny thing about her daughters. She said that we knew our mother was having clothes left from her first husband. These men's clothes were not in use—what a waste! What excess! We would put them to use and while we did so, give our nicer things away to this charity. *Masha'allah*!

It was not finished. With a flamboyant reentry, Mama withdrew a box from the top of the tall, bedroom dresser. Opening it released a small cloud of dust and a bad, musty smell. She demonstrated our new normal by dressing herself right on the spot with trousers a color unpleasantly like burnt lentils and a buttoned shirt to match. She tossed garments into our unwilling arms one-by-one.

Fahad began to snort and cackle. He shrieked with laughter, despite Auntie's shrewd, warning gaze.

I was the first to give in, and I pleaded with our mother. I led her to where we had hidden Fahad's clothing. Only, she thanked me gleefully and explained that now we could be united in our new menswear as a whole family. Fahadi practically squealed.

The shameful charade lasted until the late hours of the following morning. Bi. Mwinyi, who has always served—if unenthusiastically—as co-conspirator to our mother's tricks, she entered through the courtyard and returned our blouses, our skirts, and our *shungi* to the living room. Overcome with relief and shame, Dauda actually embraced her.

This is how Mama and Bi. Mwinyi were, too. Our mother played the master of ceremonies, the deejay, the boisterous soldier while Bi. Mwinyi was the usher, the hostess, or the human rights lawyer. Still, even as the kinder conspirator, she was having that habit of somehow sneaking away with flour or eggs. She still does this, but much less often. In fact, that day when she returned our clothes to us, I think she did leave with a *boflo* bread or two. That one! She shares everything, it is true; but she shares it right back to herself, too.

Now that our mother has gone, Bi. Mwinyi takes from our kitchen less. Even though Dauda still sucks her teeth prudishly, she has hardened. She is not one to play tricks on Fahadi anymore. And Fahadi, he cries less often. He has fewer tearful moments, but he also has fewer moments with us in general. In dull moments, when thoughts might betray us and lead back to old times Fahad takes to endless walking and discovering stray creatures. Dauda, she has no dull moment. She is always busy with some necessary task at home. And me, I suppose I go and watch the interesting people.

It is true, while Mama was here I was not as keen to record notes about the ones I see. This, it is a new hobby. I was writing in notepads and journals, but I wrote unimportant things. These things were about school and the conversations Asha, Khadija, and I had while we sat at Kiwimbi. They were not unusual or interesting things. They were only about me, really.

When I was writing in those journals, I did not look outward to the people of Unguja. I was not making observations and reading others. But, perhaps this is alright, too. Carefully watching others and learning their stories has brought me suffering! Here I am with nothing to show for it. Here I am writing about myself once again.

However, this time is different. I write about me, but here on this page Mama joins me. Dauda, Fahadi, even Auntie, they are here. They are present because they are part of who, why, where, how, and what I am. My name is Tatu because Mama gave it to me. I am a girl who lives on Unguja, in Kikwajuni near a beach named Kiwimbi, because Mama was a girl living on Unguja, in Kikwajuni, before me.

While I sit here facing the sea I wear a headscarf and cover my hair. I write with my right hand, and I have prayed when I woke up. I will pray again at noon. This is how I am, and it is because Mama has taught me to be, and Auntie reminds me to be.

I like *biriyani* because Mama would make it on special occasions. Auntie and Dauda, they do not make it like this, so it remains special to me. Unlike many girls I know, I even like cats because I am so accustomed to seeing them around our home, thanks to Fahadi. I am not late for school and I am quite good at the washing because Auntie has taught me what is wrong. Like this, they have all contributed to me.

If Mama, Auntie, Dauda, and Fahad have all contributed to me, certainly so has Bi. Mwinyi—so have Mzee Amir and Bwana Usi. Have others done so? Mzee Kahawa, the nasty boys who made violent plans, the *mzungu* who runs and gives gifts—have they influenced me? But, I only meant to watch them. Mama and my family have made me who I am, but this is sensible because they are my family. Bi. Mwinyi, she is our neighbor, so that is sensible, too, but these ones who do not know me—have they changed me?

I like to carefully watch these interesting people. I think this is because I do not find myself to be interesting. Inside of me, there is only grief for a version of me that included our mother—for a version that included a Dauda who played with other girls and a Fahadi who stayed home; for a version that did not include beatings from Auntie, but only beatings from Mama. In dull moments, when thoughts betray me, I long for the time before great, terrible accidents. It is not fair.

Auntie reminds me—and even Mama might say the same—that Allah has a plan. Everything that happens, He has a plan, and we must trust him. There are tests laid out for us, but we must trust him and stay strong. Just, it does not feel fair.

Inside me there is a grief. There has been for many months now. Unlike other ladies, I did not release it with wailing on that day the ferry boat sank. I held it inside, waiting for something that did not exist. This is why it hurt me. This is why my belly twisted up and my shoulders ached with suspicious, tense feelings.

I am done with that. For me, I will not hide from the memories of Mama now. I may not speak them, but I hold them here inside me. I have plenty of good memories which are quite interesting.

I will not hide from memories—good ones and bad ones—and so, too, I will not be so vigilant all the time. Sometimes, it is good to focus on daily tasks, but not so much that it blocks out all other things. Likewise, it is good to be carefree but not so much that I forget to care about important things.

I may not be a wave or a fish. I may not be rigid or free. I am just what I am: a girl on an island. I may look at the sea, but it is not the only thing I do. I observe the interesting people around me, but it is not because I am dull.

In fact, I will not stop this habit. I can learn what is to be understood about Kikwajuni and Unguja through observing it. But, I do not think I can continue to do it without being part of it. I am here in one place with the ones I see. I cannot pretend otherwise. We all live here together.

All together, we wake up to a new day and a new month.

This Holy Month is for cleansing. We discipline ourselves and surrender ourselves to our Creator's will. We burn away the unkind parts of ourselves, and we return to that which makes us good.

This month is for understanding physical pain. We fast and understand what it is to feel without. While we limit our bodies, we are better connecting with our spirits.

Thus, this month is for being more than a body, but also a spirit, whole.

Despite some accidents, I think I am off to a good start.

SATURDAY AFTERNOON

A DEEP EXHALATION OF BREATH escapes me, and an even deeper intake replaces it. This breath feels whole. It soothes me, and the strength of my lungs brings me confidence in my place here on a bench at Kiwimbi.

With this breath, relief envelops me. Likewise, feelings of hypervigilance—of tension and anxiety–they are alleviated. At least, they lighten. I am less burdened. Do you recall my description of bad spirits and their way of digging into shoulders and making homes there? As I gently close my new notepad, my shoulders are—well, they are just shoulders. Nothing grips me. Teeth no longer chatter in my ears.

In my heart, I have known a daily panic. I have avoided all mention of our mother, as you know. Now still, I do not recite her name. Allah has taken her, and with her goes her sacred name. Panicked heart or not, I do not alter that custom.

My breath and my heart do seem to have transformed today. They are at once lighter and stronger. I am lighter and stronger. I am calm. I might be more confident, but oh, perhaps that is yet to be determined.

Well, why not determine it? Yes, I think I shall.

Let my story not be the only one to live in this new book. Let me seek the stories of the ones I see—at Kiwimbi and Jaws Corner, in Kikwajuni and in Stonetown. I want to do for my neighbors what I have done for me. I mean to say, if committing time to telling my whole story can bring me this calmness, it can achieve the same for others. About this, I already feel confident.

These stories, I cannot know them without asking—without listening patiently. I recognize this now. Apart from perhaps Auntie, Dauda, and Bi. Mwinyi, no one knows my story. No one knows it in its fullness. How can they without listening? They cannot.

They may know that I am from Unguja, but do they know where I like to sit on cool July evenings? Kiwimbi beach is as much part of my spirit as any place in Zanzibar. They may surmise that I have two siblings, but do they know that I have a third? Yes, we are an unconventional family with different daddies—mainlander, islander, Malay—but our mother's love unites us. They may even know that I like to watch many people and ponder their stories, but do they know why? I love my neighbors, the ones I see around me. They make me who I am by being who they are. I understand them because I am one of them. Many of us, we are like the bland, maize porridge. A few of us, we are like special *biriyani*: we are rare. These rare and unusual ones inspire me. They are evidence that there is not one way of being. There are as many ways as there are people. *Duniani kuna watu*, we say; 'in the world there are people.'

In this same way, I see now that I cannot know a full person just by looking carefully. For this, I have a talent. But, even a talent for watching does not lead to understanding. Very good guesses are still guesses. If I want to understand a person's story with its boring parts and its rare parts—its good and its bad—then I must do more than watch.

Do I start with Mzee Kahawa? Do I search for the *mzungu* who runs at Kiwimbi, like he has searched for me this morning? Surely, the boys who make plans have a story to tell, but forgive me, I do not think I am not the one to record it for them. They have a very different style of storytelling which I am not ready for—much louder and with bold, red letters. For now, I prefer my stories not to provoke bombs and gases. Forgive me for my timidity.

This is different work, too. Of course, I am used to looking carefully at the ones around me, as does a detective. This that I want to do now—it is not a matter of watching, but of listening. I suppose they are similar. Both tasks require focus. Watching carefully and listening carefully, they both require me to decide what is worth recording. When I am note-taking, however, I am in control. To think about opening myself to a full story, controlled by its speaker, this feels unpredictable. This feels like vulnerability for both speaker and listener.

On the other hand, when I have written my own story just now it feels greater than vulnerability. It feels honest. Hm, this word is not enough. It feels true. Well, that is the same thing, isn't it? I tell you, giving my story to paper makes me feel that I am worthy. I am worthy of ink and of paper. I am worthy of the time it takes to recount a full story. My good parts and my bad parts, they are real and true.

If I feel vulnerable in asking for another's story then it is a thing I accept so long as that person feels worthy, too. I want to share this feeling. I will trade my vulnerability for their worthiness. To be truthful with you, I also want to do what I have always done. That is, I want to fill up my notepad with unusual and interesting things! I have looked carefully and have made observations which tell me people's stories. You know, perhaps asking is actually easier. I have not considered it this way: I do not have to do any of the work of observing and determining the truth of things. Just, I will listen. The storyteller will determine their own truth. That seems simple to me.

Again, who to solicit these stories from—stories I have not heard, perhaps delicately personal, even? Perhaps, like watching, it is a matter of going outside and finding interesting people. In this moment again, I cannot stop from wishing our mother were with us. She is the first person I would like to hear. She would always have stories—clever ones, funny ones, embarrassing ones. She could tell you all about the things that matter to us people on Unguja, too. She was knowing the things which were unusual and interesting just as much as the usual things which are interesting.

You see, now that I allow myself to remember—really remember—I recall this about her. Maybe I should have learned this from her. But, I was young when the boat sank and our mother disappeared. I was not thinking about so many things. I was not yet looking at people so carefully and writing about what I saw. In fact, I was more like Khadija and Asha. I was speaking and laughing more than looking or listening.

If our mother could tell me stories, I would fill this little notepad in just one day, oh! I tell you, she had lessons for us in her tales. When I was lazy, she would tell me about a different girl who was lazy like me and the bad things that happened to her. When I was stubborn, she had stories of stubborn monkeys who were so very stubborn until the day their stubbornness led them right into the open mouths of crocodiles.

If our mother could tell me stories today, this task would be very easy. And, I do not think she would be difficult to persuade, no. Just, I might tell her that I would like to write it down in my new, little book, and she would say *Now, this girl, enh she is a clever one. She is going to be a writer like Shafi Adam Shafi! like Shaaban Robert!* She would say a thing like that even though she rarely read books. She was knowing their names, but not their contents, you see.

Anyway, our mother is not here.

Unfortunately, Auntie is less keen on stories. If I want to start easy, she is not my first subject. Auntie will call me *mtundu* and tell me to stop playing games or else become useless like Fahadi. That is her view. Perhaps Bi. Mwinyi! She has told me things about spirits who live in baobab trees and young ladies who disappear into caves. Thus, I know she has stories to tell. As I think on it, though, she has never offered stories about herself. Though, I have never asked for one directly before.

However, it is worth a try! Let me see if Bi. Mwinyi is home.

I rise up and make my way across the airport road. Kikwajuni is sleepy this afternoon. Ramadhan has begun, and on a Saturday, too. There are no classes for learners to attend. Far fewer people do their exercises at Kiwimbi. They are probably preserving their energy.

Even the airport road is all but empty. I barely look to either side before crossing it. I enter Kikwajuni where Mzee Ameir's house stands. This morning, he is not sitting on his stoop. Probably, he is at mosque, or perhaps inside resting ahead of a long day of fasting. This trend continues as I make my way down the unpaved road. Even the chickens, they languish under a jasmine bush. Everyone knows that today is a day of slow, calm reflection. Few are out in the street.

Despite this, I spy Bi. Mwinyi hunched over a patch of sweet potato greens. She is an active lady and not one to rest late into mornings, even today. She plucks at the leaves, preparing some sauce for when we break the fast tonight. I hope she shares it. Usually, neighbors take turns sharing what they have made. Those greens are not as exciting as *biriyani*, sure, but they are very delicious in their way. Bi. Mwinyi is known to have a heavy hand with her cumin, too. I like this.

Gathering my pen and notepad, I prepare myself mentally. Gone are the days of carefully watching. I ready myself for this new era of carefully hearing.

First, however, I step into our courtyard. This *shungi* needs washing after a particularly long week of wear. I cast it off and drop it into a basin. Draped over the line, there is a dry *kanga*, and I toss it over my hair. Not tightly, but enough to cover myself. *Mchungulia bahari si msafiri*, reads its caption: letters on a field of blue—a blue like those deep, deep parts of open sea where your feet are not even visible below you and you must know how to swim. I like its yellow stripes, lining the border. They are bold.

Scampering like one of Fahadi's clandestine kittens, I make my way nervously back through the courtyard. Dauda is boiling water for rice, and she scowls through the sides of her eyes at my commotion. Reaching the rusty, red door I close it behind me gently. Owh, but Bi. Mwinyi is preoccupied with her greens. Perhaps I am too quiet.

On the other hand, I do not wish to startle her. That would start on the wrong foot. And, my feet are walking on new ground as it is. I think it is better to gain her attention with some common sound than with a voice attached to me. Thus, I reopen the door just a little, and I close it with more purpose this second time.

The rusted metal scrapes and squeals. Bi. Mwinyi turns slightly to see what causes such noise, and my plan has worked. Her attention is peeked, but she is not agitated by a sudden invader. Doors squeak all the time; it is interesting, but not at all startling. My fanfare of aged aluminum announces me, and Bi. Mwinyi sees me exiting the doorway. Now, I can greet her naturally.

"*Shikamoo, bibi.*"

"*Marahaba, mwanangu,*" she replies. "What is that you have?"

She acknowledges my notepad. I smile.

"This, it is like a book, *bibi*," and I add, "I fill it with stories."

"What kind of stories?"

"Any kind! My stories and yours, important ones and little, everyday ones."

Her eyes widen, and her mouth narrows doubtfully.

"*Hebu*, you want to put my words into that book?"

I click my tongue in agreement.

"My child, how can you put what I say into writing? I tell you many stories. Why do you want them on paper now? You are going to cause me trouble, now. I do not want it."

I sigh disappointedly, and take her hand gently in my own. I should have known that this would not be so easy.

"*Bibi*! No one reads my stories. You are not going to have trouble!"

"No one reads what you write in your book—child, what sort of book is not meant for reading?"

"Owh, well, it is for reading, but I am the only one who reads it, Bi. Mwinyi. And—and, it is not just the reading. It is for writing, and for listening. Just, I want to know what you think is worth hearing."

Bi. Mwinyi looks slightly impressed now. I know this because she does not immediately reply. Like most Swahili ladies, Bi. Mwinyi has all the answers and many words. In this moment, though, she withholds them. This highlights the unusual nature of my plan. I do not think anyone has ever shared an idea like this one with her before.

After a meaningful silence, "You are going to write all the words I say?"

"Ah, *bibi*, not every word, but just all the things which are important."

"Aren't all my things important, *we*?"

This makes me giggle. Bi. Mwinyi's words have returned to her now.

"Listen, you can watch me as I write, if you like. It is not secret work. If I have forgotten something important, you will interrupt me, *bibi*."

"Mmh," she nods approvingly.

"*Haya, bibi.*"

I pause as I think about what it is that I want to say next. I have not done this before. Now, I am sailing in new waters.

"Bi. Mwinyi, please. Tell me what it is like to be you."

ABOUT THE AUTHOR

TIMOTHY HOFFELDER is an *mzungu* who grew up in southwestern Pennsylvania, near Pittsburgh. His education at Indiana University took him to Zanzibar, Tanzania, where he studied Swahili, lived with a Zanzibari family, and worked with his local colleagues to produce educational resources. He maintains contacts there, including his host family and his friend Bart, a local painter who created the cover art for *Who Only Looks at the Sea*. Currently, Timothy lives in the West Town area of Chicago, Illinois.

CPSIA information can be obtained
at www.ICGtesting.com
Printed in the USA
BVHW03s1931050918
526617BV00001B/70/P